Elizabeth's City

a novella

by Kevin Rabas

Spartan Press
Kansas City, Missouri
spartanpresskc.com

Also by Kevin Rabas:

Bird's Horn
Lisa's Flying Electric Piano
Spider Face
Sonny Kenner's Red Guitar
Green Bike (with Simmons & Graves)
Eliot's Violin
Songs for My Father
All That Jazz
Late for Cymbal Line
Like Buddha-Calm Bird
Everyone Just Wants to Drum
Watch Your Head
On Drums

Elizabeth's City

We bought a six pack of Boone's fruity, diluted drinks, and we sat and laughed. Her smile was back. Then, she cried when she showed me the notes and transcripts from the shrinks, what they had said. She laid them out on the hotel bed, and they were in yellows, pinks, and greens, pieces of carbon marked paper, the pen pushing the purple ink through. These were her copies.

There were two beds. Later that night, we would make love. It would be my first time with anyone. This is what she wanted. She wanted healing. She'd done so much of it, and here I was, the one around to do it now for her.

She'd only been there a few days. I picked her up at the coffee shop, and all of her things were in two large brown grocery bags. Clothes spilled over the top, pinks and reds and tans. She said she was going to sleep in the park, and I said, "No. Come with me." I don't know if there was love there anymore for us, but we were familiar, and a flame burned down low and only needed the turn of a knob, the touch of a hand, to rise up and fill both of our bodies with heat.

Liz was disheveled, but beautiful. Her eyes moved a lot, tracking. It was as if she had been hunted for too long, and now she couldn't come down, calm down. I put my hand on her waist, something I had not done for her or any girl, and she settled. She leaned into me and wrapped her arms around my body. Her head went up, and she leaned back, arching. She wanted to kiss, and we did. We walked to my car, I started it, and we left the coffee shop parking lot, headed west across Westport to the Holiday Inn. I had never taken a girl to a hotel before.

It all began earlier at a gig. A jazz gig in Kansas City, city of youth. Months ago, I met Liz. She was in the front row, head thrown back, her red hair a marigold mane, and she was laughing and smoking and eyeing me like I was dinner—or dessert. I was playing in Ryan Parks' trio, eclectic and straight-ahead jazz. We gathered every Saturday night at 8 at 51st Street Coffee House, a stone's throw from UMKC and a short walk from where I used to have an apartment, until a month ago, when I moved back in with my parents. I drove my blue Blazer and parked at the sidewalk and haul in my drums, red Gretches that shone in the city lights like Liz's blazing hair, spun in ringlets like Molly Ringwald's in *Pretty in Pink*, and Liz had that same laughing scowl, that neo-Beat frown that said, "This ain't good, but it's good enough, for now."

Ryan had come off a bender, and when Billy Dee set his Guinness glass on Ryan's blonde corduroy amp I thought Ryan was going to haul off and sock Billy Dee. Instead, Ryan kicked "Cherokee" at break-neck speed, maybe quarter note equals 360, and had Billy start with a solo across vibes. Billy Dee had just dragged in his silver slatted instrument along with a menagerie of hand percussion, nestled beside me and my small coffee shop kit, drum set picked to play this little metal-roofed room. Too loud, and the boss man would first open the door wide, let night air and street light in, then he'd motion with a hand: "Down, lower. Lower." Billy schlepped his stuff in a big white van, off the road from an indie band tour, back in town, playing this gig for kicks. So, we're three: drums, percussion, and big brown upright bass. Sometimes, wind instruments sit in. Ryan's got us playing some trumped up version of the bridge of "Cherokee," with its stampede of low notes, my sticks along the low tom, bass drum thumping, and Liz's rising in her seat and falling, rocking, riding the rhythms, and I can't quit thinking of how sexy this is, she is, though I haven't met her yet. This is how. When she smiles, it's like she's sucking a lemon or lime through parted teeth, sipping at rhythm. Green eyes, red hair, fair and freckled skin. Probably 20-21, I think. Alone. I've been playing this gig for a couple of months now. Never seen her before. And Ryan pulls me back in, noticing, "Your turn, James," he says. "Hit those skins," and he steps back with his bass, hand over the strings as if covering a prayer book, and Billy pulls his foot from the vibes pedal, the pedal flipping up. Nothing. Not a sound, not a note. And so I fill it. With a story. I play the low tom first, call on my heart with low notes, kettle drum roll, double- (now) single-stroke rolls, then spread across the toms, high tom and snare with the snares sprung, sometimes placing a hand or elbow to the drum and talk-drumming the head, sometimes holding the stick tip to the head and cross-stick tapping out a code, warming the room, working, boiling toward the flurry of melodic Max Roach rolls over skins. Liz bought and rocked to this rhythm, her knees and feet pumping, riding that chair. When over, she blew me a kiss. End of the set, and she was up to me. I tried to say something, but she put a hand over my lips, pushed a scrap of paper into my front pocket: "Call me. Liz: 816-316-6050 SWAK" and at the bottom there was a half-moon, brandy-colored lipstick kiss.

Twenty-four hours later, and I'm sitting at her table at 51ˢᵗ StreetCoffee, waiting. I'm a little early, so I order a chai tea with soy. I don't drink milk. The ice cubes are muddy with dark chai, and, as I sip, I watch the city sweat—the thin men in dark cyclist gear and helmets, huffing, spinning pedals, their spokes speed blurred; their sunglasses cost more than some of my drums. There're women in sun yellows and pastels, running, pushing hip, three-wheel baby strollers in front of them, running, running their figures past the men stopped at crumbling brick corners who hold cardboard signs with Sharpie pen letters: "Too ugly to prostitute. Too stoopid to steal." I wait an hour. I wait an hour more. No Liz. No girl. And then, here she comes, frazzled, sweating, as if she's run four blocks to get here. Her green flip flops are in one hand. Her hip, purple polka dotted sundress barely on, red bra straps out, crooked.

"I've got a confession, James," she says with a quick grin. But her eyes fall. Something serious.

"What is it?"

She holds my name in her mouth, like one of those over-large whiskey ice cubes. James?

"Jamie, honey, I was just with someone else."

"With?"

"Sex, preppy. Just now."

I feel the summer air roll over me, sweat. I look at her eyes, green and steady. She's serious. "Really?"

"Maybe we shouldn't be doing this, this first date. I really just want to go and clean up. Shower."

"You can." At last, I'm thinking quicker, as on the stand, seeing ahead of the changes before they come. That's what drummers do. "Maybe it's not right, we're not right. Not in the cards." She straightens the straps of her dress, runs a hand through her hair.
"So, let's play our hand," I say. "See what those cards say."
"Maybe you want some other girl."

She's not letting up. We may be done.

"Not particularly," I say. "How about we go back to your place, Elizabeth, and I wait while you shower?"

"Liz. Call me Liz. And you can't come into the shower with me. Not yet."

"Ok." I've run out of notes, the rhythm lost. But I stay right with her, listening for the pulse.

"Let me tell you something. I heal people."

"Heal people?" I wonder if she means crystals or a light blue nurse jumper?

"Yes. Through sex."

"Really?" I'm sweating, but I don't touch my brow.

"Yes. It's one of my gifts. I save guys who are down and out, spent. Through sex. I give guys a jump start." She stops, looks. I look up, try not to draw attention to the sweat running down my forehead, my neck, down my back. She's got me. "Does this turn you on or off?"

"On, I think. On," I say.

"Ever had sex?"

"Uh."

"Want to learn? Good. Let's go."

And so I meet Liz, full of magic, at 51st St, on a Sunday, hot as heck.

I buy her a pack of American Spirits, and we hit the sidewalk. She still has her shoes in her hand. Barefoot, she walks the hot sidewalk, over cig butts and yellow handbills and little blue-green scatterings of glass.

"What, no shoes?" I say.

"Unnecessary accessories. I like to feel where I walk."

"Been here long?"

"All my life. This is my city, honey."

I grew up in the suburbs. Came here for school. Never seen anything like this. Anything like her.

Her house is in Brookside, one in a row of A-frames built in the '50s. The red paint is flaking and has the texture of the brown, burnt bread rim of a piece of plastic bag toast. There's a wide porch with a swing for two and two lawn chairs with those green criss-crosses holding the metal together. It's only a three-minute walk from the coffee shop to her door. The front door's wide open with only the screen between us and the indigo dark inside. Liz tosses her shoes on the porch, takes me by the elbow, and pulls me in.

"Come on," she says. "No one's home."

Up the stairs we go, and, as we do, she plays a game, a kind of mock strip-tease, taking off her dress and plopping that fabric into my hands.

"What? Never seen ladies' underthings before?"

She unclasps her bra, but holds the apparatus on, revealing nothing, and says, "Sit," and I perch on the toilet lid.

"No peeking," she says, and off go the rest, her panties and her bra, draped over the top of the shower top. A blurred glass between us, Liz flips the shower head on hot, the white steam gathering and obscuring her figure more, but I can't help but look at her form, her curves, like the looping shapes a swan's neck makes, like the movements of dancers, silhouetted, like some hot girl in a window on Beale Street, beckoning.

"So tell me your story, preppy? I take long showers," Liz says.

I've got my hands in my lap, pulling at my fingers.

"Though I grew up in Shawnee, I'm not really preppy," I say. "My father's a construction worker, and my mom works for a small paper. I write, too."

"My daddy's got a hole in his heart."

"Really?"

"My mother tries to fill it every night."

"I'm sorry."

"Never mind," she says. "So you write *and* play jazz drums?"

"Yes."

"A real writer?"

"I guess."

"Me, too," she says.

"What kind?"

"Performance poet," she says, lifting an arm above the shower top, like a dancer in a twirl. "You?"

"I like prose," I said. "Like Tom Wolfe."

"Electric Kool Aid Acid Test?"

"Yes."

"Didn't picture you that wild," she says. "What do you do for work or do you mooch off mommy and daddy?"

"I read poetry at nursing homes."

"Pay much?"

"75 dollars a pop," I say.

"Not bad. Smooth move, preppy."

"I do 4-8 places a day."

"Contemporary work?"

"Classic poems," I say. "Things they love and know. Sometimes those old zombies even rise and recite."

"I'll bet you don't call them that. At work. Zombies."

"No," I say. "But you should see them, stiff-limbed, arms out, pacing from window to TV." I mimic the motion, bumping stiff-armed into the shower. Liz puts a hand to the glass, presses a cheek.

"Scary, dude."

"What do you do?" I ask.

"I teach old rich people how to dance. Ballroom. At EE's." Liz shuts off the shower. "Do you sing and dance?"

"Uh, no," I shrug, "not really."

"I didn't think so. Can you hand me that towel?"

I pull a thick pink towel from a hook. The towel smells like roses. When I give her the towel, her hand touches mine.

"Thanks," she says. "Wait outside."

I leave the bathroom, shut the door behind.

The floors are dark hardwood, scuffed. I hear Liz singing something while she dries.

"Somewhere Over the Rainbow." Her voice is high, soprano. Chirpy. But with a little gravel down low. Kind of like Tori Amos. Smokers. They always have that gravel, that bit of Joe Cocker, Janis Joplin phlegm. Liz doesn't take long. When she comes out, she runs a hand through my goatee.

"I like a man with one of these. Some fur on his face."

"I grew it in Germany."

"Really?" she says.

"Sister City trip. I shot a video of my town, won a contest. Winners got to go."

"Why a beard in Germany?"

"I got tired of shaving every day, on the road, on the train, carrying a thick rucksack everywhere I go. So, I let it grow."

"I like it," she says. "Maybe one day I'll let you brush up against me with your sweet goatee. Come on, loverboy," she says, "let's go meet my friend."

I drive us to Nichol's Lunch, where we sit and sip dark coffee from pale cups. Liz rims her cup with lipstick.

"My friend lives near here. He'll be along."

Down the sidewalk comes a figure in shadow, pushing a wheelbarrow slow, like a ditch digger now off for the night. As he comes closer, we can see the wheelbarrow doesn't have sand or gravel, but a thick burlap tarp over the top.

"That's Archie," Liz says, and we leave dollars on the table, flee to the door, and Archie grounds his wheelbarrow and holds out his arms, and Liz and he hug long. Archie has dark hair and dark eyes, and he is all city spiff, like the charmer character in *Trainspotting*, all flash and flair. He flips a silver Zippo to life and lights a cig for Liz, which she sips, then puts the tip to Archie's lips.

"Been too long," Archie says. "Who's this?"

"Jamie," she says.

"Your new one?"

"He's the one," she says.

She flips a corner of the tarp up, and the streetlights catch metal, caught silver, caught glint. Stereos are stacked inside, piled. A mountain of music makers.

"New stereos?" Liz says.

"You know me."

"I think you should take those back," she says. "They look more than gently used."

"Hand me downs. For impoverished artists."

"Who live with their mothers," she says.

"Now now, Liz. You don't have to rub it in. Come on, now," Archie says. "I need to get these home."

"To mama," Liz says.

"To my room."

When we get to Archie's house, the wooden door, like Liz's, is wide open. What was left was the screen. I cut ahead and open the screen door.

"Here, let me help you with that," I say.

"My crime, my heft," Archie says. "I lift. I push."

"You sure you can't use help?"

Archie tousles his hair, like a Kennedy. "I've carted these stereos five blocks, buddy. I can make it a few more feet. But if you don't mind stepping aside—"

"Sure," I say. And in he goes.

Archie's room is mood-lit low, the air like the dark mahogany wood pieces within.

Archie's room is thick with dark wood, like an antique shop set on Jay Gatsby's block, the room full of end tables and tall, slatted chairs, a chaise lounge, and an antique TV set housed in wood the hue of dark chocolate and cherry. Little lamps with yellow light illuminate the room; glass crystals hang and sway on their lamp shades; pale doilies circumscribe their lamp feet as a blanket does a Christmas tree.

I help Archie heft the first batch of stereos into the room and against a wall.

"He's helpful, sweetie," Archie says. "Where'd you find him, church?"

Liz grins and shoots back, "Archie, you know my face would start smoking if I even set foot in church. James here is a writer. Went to school for creative writing."

"Well, went, but didn't finish," I say.

"Admirable effort, bub," Archie says. "B+ for stick-to-it-ive-ness. What'd you learn?"

"How to place commas."

"Uncommon learning. Progressive school system. What brings you two to my door, dearies?"

"We thought you could use some company," Liz says.

"Actually, I've got other company coming."

"Hot date?" Liz says.

"Well, I hope he's still hot."

Someone down the corridor hears us talking and says, "Archibald Winters, that you?"

"Yeah, Mom," he says. "Back from stacking the trash."

"It better be trash, young man."

"Always is. Always is."

"Archie's an artist," Liz says. "You'll see. He turns stereos and trash into treasures."

"Neat," I say.

"Better than neat," says Archie. "It's all art."

"So about this man," Liz says. "Where'd you meet him?"

"At the Writer's Den. He was serving hors d'oeuvres from a shiny silver plate. Pate. I almost licked it from his fingers."

"Writer's Den. Sounds like your kind of place," says Liz. "Wine and cheese. Sports jackets and slacks. Cocktail dresses and pearls. The hairflip, the nod, the turn-away elbow or shoulder."

I shrug. "I used to volunteer there, but I wouldn't say I'm *in* there. I guess I'm just not country club enough."

"Oh, come on, preppy," Liz says.

In the distance, a drone, much like the rise of summer cicadas rises, slow and melodic at first, then grating. The sound of blue and red sirens circles the street, circles the block, circles the city.

"That ain't for me," says Archie.

"You sure?"

"Sure."

Archie takes a tan tarp and covers his stereos, tucking the edges in along the wall.

"So, how long have you two lovebirds known each other?" he says.

"First date," Liz says.

Archie says, "So, what do you think, preppy?"

"I'm lucky. To be with her. An intelligent, passionate woman. An artist, poet."

"Well said," says Archie. "That's her." And he puts an arm around her. She hugs him back. "He's not bad," Archie says.

"Told ya," said Liz. "He's a keeper." She pulls away, says, "Now show Jamie here what you do with your loot."

"Wanna see?" he says.

I say, "Sure."

"Archie's a real artist," Liz says. "An assembler. A collagist of technology."

"You see," Archie says, "I take these antique shells, like this upscale 1940s hardwood TV casing and place modern components in them, like this DVD player and modern screen. I keep the original TV bubble on, but behind it, state of the art. Stately art. Notice how this Victrola has a CD player inside. The true sound of this terrier-mix to listen to, the sound of its modern master."

"Brilliant!" says Liz.

"Sure is."

"And an ingenious way to purpose borrowed goods," Archie says.

A man in his 20s buzzes in, hair all moussed up, black leather jacket and tattoos and white-washed jeans. He smiles a crooked grin. No one seems to notice that he's come in through the door to a house he's never known.

"Hi there, gorgeous," Archie says. "So good to see you. Burge, right? With the lovely silver platter." Archie's laying it on thick.

"You got it, sweets. I'm here to serve."

"Strong name, Burge."

And Burge flexes, his leather jacket creaking. "I'm a strong man."

"I can see that. Excuse us, friends," Archie says and takes Burge's arm and leads the big man into the living room.

"So, Archie's a thief?" I say.

Liz frowns. She twirls a lock of her curly red hair. "Please don't judge," she says.

"Besides art, it's what he does best."

"Lives with his mom?"

"A kind of deal he made with the judge. Live at home until 18, instead of juvie." She holds her wrists out, as if cuffed, then behind her back. "Remember that Kriegle's diamond heist last year?"

"Who wouldn't?"

"Archie did that on a dare. But his eyes were bigger than his pockets. He got caught."

"Seems like he's picked up where he left off."

"Oh, that's just small stuff. Pocket change," Liz says.

"Do you ever help him?"

"No. I just steal kisses." And she kisses me, quick, on the cheek.

"That's my kind of theft."

"Ok. I'll close my eyes, and let's see if you can kiss me gently enough that I don't know where you're kissing," Liz says with a grin. She's a little girl again.

"Ok. Deal." This could be fun.

I kiss her lightly on the elbow. She doesn't shudder.

"Elbow. Too easy. Try again."

I bend, and, as I do, I see the length of her, her body in full taken in snapshots, in segments, in pieces as René Magritte reveals in his surrealist paintings, how the eye can only see so much at once, and so we construct the body as one, once we have seen each piece, each shot. I settle on her ankle, give her a butterfly kiss, light as an eyelash wink.

"Better. Ankle," she says.

I rise, slowly, her body an ocean to pass over, and I kiss her on the forehead.

"Way too easy. Forehead," she says. "No lines there, you might notice."

"No worries?"

"Not many."

I grow bolder, sink, kiss her with quiet passion on the lips, my lips pulling hers, a swell, a tug.

"I wondered when you'd get around to that," she says.

We kiss longer. Can we match? There are few ways better to know than a kiss. That first kiss, like a first glance, can sum up a lifetime, a love, like a hand going into a glove. Does it fit?

"Not bad," she says. "My turn."

I close my eyes, and I wait. I feel her breathing on my cheek, and then her kiss, not a bit tentative, like a bite and not a nibble. She knows what she wants.

"Ear," I say.

She kisses again, her breath first a wave upon my forehead, hair. The hairs sift in the wind of her breath, pampas plumes in Kansas wind.

"Forehead," I say.

"Yours is wrinkly," she says. "What are you worried about?" And then, though I cannot see her, I sense her grin, her mocking smirk. "Is the rest of you this way?" she says.

"Uh."

"Guess we'll have to find out."

And now she's close, her breath on my mouth, my nose, and she dives, her head along my body, past my pecs, past my navel, and then all stops. Sirens ring out loud all around us, up close, and her head is at my neck, and my eyes bolt open, and she shucks.

"The cavalry," she says.

And someone bursts through the door. It's Burge, Archie's guy, and he's patting his wallet pocket, like he just got paid.

"That was quick," Liz blurts.

And Burge pulls something out of his front pocket, cat-quick. A switchblade. Time stops, and Liz and I freeze. I take her shoulder and pull her behind me. My chest puffs. My fists clench, then loosen, something from karate. I was no good at kata, but was good at sparring. One more moment, and I can be on him.

But he chuckles, flips the blade, and combs back his hair with black plastic teeth. Not a blade, but a comb.

"Oh, I thought that was something else," Liz says.

"He said take any of these here stereos I want," Burge says, lifting the tarp and hefting a stereo onto his shoulder, and out he goes, a black and silver flash.

"See ya," he says.

Archie rushes in.

"Did he get away?" Archie says.

"Just now," Liz says. "And with one of your stereos."

"And my wallet. Frickin' thief." Archie's disheveled, his pants and shirt thrown quickly on, the buttons off, his hair a ruffled mess. He runs a hand through his hair, tugs at his buttons.

"Guess there's no honor among thieves," Liz jokes.

"Honor, my ass," says Archie. "He's all up on me, kissing me, then pulls out … a knife."

"I'm sorry, sweetie." She puts an arm 'round him.

"That turn-coat. That user. That frickin' waiter," Archie spits.

"You know, there's only one letter that separates a writer from a waiter?" I say.

"Which one?" Liz says.

I pull my notepad from my front pocket and write, "Change the "a" to an "r", and there you have it," I say, drawing the figure out: *Waiter/ Writer*. Archie scans the letters and blinks.

"Very funny," he says. "But that one, I can assure you, can't write. Can't spell. Can't kiss. Can't—"

"I hear ya," says Liz. "Sorry, Archie." She hugs him tight. "They're not all artists and thieves."

"But that's the kind I like," says Archie.

"Well, you're not stealing this one from me," she says, putting an arm around me. "I'm keeping him."

"Don't I get a say?" I say.

"No. I'm stealing you. Now." She grabs hold of me, then pulls us all into a big group hug. She's warm to the touch.

"You, I'm just borrowing, Archie. But know I'm coming back. Jamie, you're with me, tonight. We've even sealed it with a kiss. Come on," she says, and she takes my hand and leads me to the door.

"Go on, you breeders," says Archie.

"Don't worry, Archie. You'll find a better thief," Liz says. "Or maybe an artist, next."

Archie says, "Honey, we artists are all thieves."

Into the night we go. I drive to 51st Street Coffee, and we have quick drinks, and Liz says, "Let's walk the rest to my house, the long way," and we do, hand in hand, past Loose Park, full of roses on trellises and fountains and pads of grass. Also, there's the long sidewalk and blacktop ribbons that front the lake, and we walk these in the streetlamp light. Not long, and we are upon strings of words written in rainbow-colored chalk, the characters just large enough to make out in the night's lamplight glow. I've seen these before. I ran them mornings while I was at UMKC in "Fitness Running," a PE credit I needed to graduate. Wake at 6 and eat, then run 8-9, huff along. I have a touch of asthma, and the teacher would always ask, "How you makin' it, James?" And I'd say, "Fine, coach." "Carry on," he'd say, shake his head, and maybe think, "Hope this one doesn't die on my watch." I'd be safe, though. The med school's big at UMKC. Lots of type-A, wanna-be doctors would be running alongside, thin and pert and smart and driven by ambition, position, and riches.

"Look," I say. "Sidewalk chalk poetry."

"Aiden's. Aiden Kirschbaum's."

"You know him?"

"I know just about everybody in Midtown."

"Really?" I say.

"Really," and she squeezes my hand harder.

I stoop, her hand a tether, a fishing line, and read, "' My love, I pray I have not cheapened you with my words, my hands, my lips.' What crap," I say.

"At least he loves someone."

"Or lusts after someone," I say. I look into Liz's green eyes.

"Even lust is an underdeveloped form of love," she says. "Give him time."

"He's in his fifties. He's had time."

"Maybe not enough."

"Do you have lust?" she says.

"For who? You?"

"Yes."

"I just met you," I say.

"So?"

"Yes," I say. "I admit it. Yes."

"What are you going to do about it?"

"I don't know. Kiss you?" And I go to, but she pulls back.

"I have an idea," she says. "Write about it."

"In chalk? On the sidewalk?"

"No, silly," she says. "On me."

"What?" Liz pulls a Sharpie pen from a pocket and hikes up her long skirt a bit, to reveal her ankle and part of her leg.

"Write about it here," she says.

"On you?"

"Yes. Before you forget."

"But what should I write?"

"Whatever comes."

"But what if you don't like it?" I say.

"That's your risk. You want to woo a girl, write well."

And I write. And I watch the rises and falls in her body, the gentle jitters of the flesh, the landmark veins, pale blue-green beneath the chalky stretches of skin, smooth sailing my Sharpie over those flat expanses, like bodies of soundless water, including the blood and muscle, bones, we cannot see, but which stitch and ligament us together, the skeleton, like a soul, beneath, the tree and branches beneath the leaves. I write and write, each word like a gemstone in haiku, then end with: "I want to write all over your body. Fill every space."

And she says, "You can't."

And I say, "Why not?"

And she pulls her skirt up, revealing other black lines and loops of script, tattoo-like and expansive as tattoo arm sleeves, lots of minutes and moments spent etching script across skin, others here first, others here all over, their hands on her pale skin.

"Look at all of this writing. Who wrote all of this?"

"Some of it's mine," she says. "Some, other guys. A few, other women. You're not the only one," she says. "But you're the only one I want right now," and she kisses me quick on the forehead, like a master complimenting a student, golden dojo touch.

"Want?"

"Your words," she says, "on my body. That's what I want. Then, I want to touch you, and what I want is soundless: penned words and your lips."

And then she unbuttons my shirt, quick, as a nurse would or a woman in a bodice-ripped paperback, and I do not move, do not protest, but wait as one would who was being buzzed by a sweat bee, wanting not to be stung or struck.

I let a "hey" escape, a whisper.

"Shh," she says. "You know, I'm only the first. In time, lots of other women will write all over you."

We kiss, long, my mind winding into the past and the future on a red thread, like a strand of Liz's hair, but endless, strung like a Rapunzel lock, the curls gone, pulled straight like a looping phone line cord. In the past, I see Liz rocking to the tunes, her chair a rocking horse, her hips in rhythm to my hi-hat, her heart one of my drums: thump-thump, thump-thump, she plays me. The future, I will save for later, but she is large in the belly, with our child, a hand on the hump, hill, a hand draped in mother love, a hand ringed and shining, with a diamond, one bigger than I could really give her, but wished I could. Was it mine?

When I pull up beside his parents' house, Lean has a desktop computer tower in his arms, the black tower glistening, glowing in the sun.

Lean is in his work-shirt polo, branded with his name, "LEAN," in cursive white along the spot a patch would be in a button-up, and Lean spends his weekends and nights in that red-orange shirt. A hardware man in a world that is turning to software, a world full of Micro-serfs in California, so many states away, but even here in the Midwest, in Kansas, Lean has a place, a plot of programming land, sand turned to computer wafers, to chips, not unlike the things Pac-Man chomped on decades before, when Lean and I were little, playing at the screen until our black plastic consoles overheated and we had to stop for the day, our parents saying things like, "It's like your video games, son. You have to keep at it, play until you know." My father would say that about plumbing, hammering nails, about fiddling with the car. I had had a white '67 Mustang Fastback back then, a go-fer for my father's tools and dreams, best car, coolest, hippest car, I knew I would ever own. My dream, my father's. The girls I found, because of that car. Their lipstick kisses on my far window, on my car body all because of my father, his tastes, his latent loves. Father was good for more than one thing. What he loved endured, decades.

"What's all this?" I say.

And Lean says, "It's for our game tonight. "LAN party."

"LAN party?"

"Local Area Network."

"Network." Lean could see I didn't get it.

"To the layman," said Lean, "a bunch of computers hooked, so you can fight it out together, here, in my parent's basement. LAN."

"I see."

"You still dazed about that girl," he says. "Aren't you?"

"Dazed?"

"Can't focus on the real, can you?" he says. "You been with her yet?"

"What?"

"Do the wild thing?"

"No." I laugh.

"Why not?"

"You been with anyone?"

"No. But close. She got nice tits?"

"Haven't seen them."

"Touched them?"

"No."

"What *are* you doing, kissing?"

"Sure."

"As my dad would say, 'Get with the program, son.'"

"It's not like that."

"It needs to be," he says. "Don't play with her. And don't play with me, telling me about it."

"Ok," I say. "I hear ya."

"Well, get a move on," and he hands me a tower. "And help me carry these inside."

Lean's house is a modest split-level ranch, all wood with no brick out front like the others on the block, that red and white striped brick that says we're moving up, and in through the garage we go, a clutter-free garage that holds two cars and a metal shelf full of Snapple bottles, his father's stash, and sometimes Lean and Lean's brother, Adam, and I would drink from that, maybe find a full potato chip bag on the shelf, and feast like teens do, eating upon air, upon salt and sugar and nothing good, but this afternoon we plug in cords downstairs in the dimness of those teenage years, in that extra time we were wont to waste in those electric pixels, the first wave of kids to spend our days within screens, within the depths of plastic and silica, within the depths of something we could not see grow, but it did, and soon the world was one big LAN gathering, kids holding plastic or tapping their typing fingers across keys, eyes captured by what the network had become: one big training ground, training gig for the cubicle and the military sand-expanse tent, one lasting hypnotic game, trance for the lower and middle classes.

I go see Liz. When I knock on her door, I hear Liz's hand on a padlock she has inside on a u-shaped hinge, her hands spinning it, fingers against the dial, fingers against metal, the quick, chirpy sound of a worn-out lock, but she knows what she's doing, doesn't take long dialing the numbers as one would on a rotary phone. The moment lasts because I find it peculiar, her using a lock like that on a door that has a knob, something here she's improvised, something she's done to turn a house full of a family into a family that has a hanger-on, her, grown as she sees it, she's still there and not there, a renter in her childhood home.

She grins, but her smile is muted when I see her, and when I look down I see the reason. She's in pink panties, ripple-like wrinkles in them, since she's been sleeping. I can see it in her eyes, her top eyelids a little drooped, and she has nothing else on, her breasts a little longer than I had expected, pale, drooped, long and thin, like white tube socks, but sexier, and the tips so pink, like strawberries dipped in cream, and she sees me noticing, studying, and says, " 'bout time," and, "There's more," and she kisses me, hijacking my face and pulling me into the room and shutting the door without latching it, and soon we're on the floor on her mattress along one wall, and she has my shirt off, and then my khakis, rumpled 'round my ankles, and I wonder is this it, is this how it happens, my first time, and the kissing's turned to a flurry of thousand hands, like the tantric god and goddess statues I've seen at the Nelson, museum around the corner, down the block, up Rockhill Road, where somewhere, sometime someone raided the Asian temples and brought their statues to a new home in KC, and at night I hear Charon Eismann shines a light on their faces looking for halo glow; there are gods in our midst, and they pet and scrump each other under those old-style skirts.

Somehow I get her underpants off in the melee of hands and kisses, in shifts of position; we do not roll, but we might if we were slower, and so I'm above her, and I follow her curves down to a reddish swatch of hair, not much but something, rust colored, amber wheat-colored. I've never known a red head this close, this far, this deep, and I put my mouth to her lower lips, and she sighs, and her head goes back, and then she shifts, banshee-quick, and I feel her hands turn to claws, and she runs one finger deep into my back, a slash, and my mind knows her hands say "NO," and she stops me quick as a cat-scratch across linoleum, a skitter and a stop, and I bolt up, and I go to her face shrinking, and say, "Hey, I—. What's up?"

"You are, preppy. Were. I'm warning you."

"About?"

"This. You ever done this before?"

"No. So? Am I that bad? So, I—"

"So, if you don't know where a girl's been, you shouldn't do that."

"Do what?"

"Eat a girl out."

"Why?"

"Diseases."

"Have any?"

"Don't know, but might, trigger. Might."

And, like that, night closes in upon us, through the window, a black moon-less night, and we hold like children might after a twister or a thick slate storm, thankful the rain and wind have gone, as water, as ice, and what you hold more than anything is the self, the lost lost self, alive but broken and scattered by wind and rain.

When we wake from this moment, Liz is lit like a Christmas light bulb that climbs to its highest brightness after a moment or two of light, shining bright as it can.

"Let's go to the slam at Grinder's," she says. "Up for it?"

"But first, coffee," she says. And her hand has my hand, and we are back in the night, she barefoot, me in my mountain boots I always wear, in khakis and in jeans and in church slacks, something I learned in scouts and out about town, wear footwear that can go over dirt or grass or blacktop, sidewalk.

"Get me a double-espresso, trigger," Liz says. "I'll get us a table."

We're at Broadway Café, longest-standing coffee shop on this block. Starbucks tried a bout, parked right next to this local, and the die-hard townies just kept coming in the door of Broadway, in droves in flocks in herds, and eventually Starbucks stepped back, gave in and left, found another town. Even the *Times* covered it: the locals win. Even New York knew, the small and homegrown sometimes makes a place, even in big-time boom times, when Ben Franklin hobbies busts its breast-shirt buttons and hulks into Walmart, the big fish, the narwhal, the shark to all that is homegrown, homey, and small.

I'm in the line a time, minutes, an expanse, behind hipsters in blue tats in mechanic shirts with others' names on the lapels in overalls in lumberjack red and black-checkered plaid with the sleeves pinking-sheared off, in jean cutoffs, Daisy Dukes, in blue hair, in purple, in tube shirts and black leather with chrome studs, in army green rucksacks pre-faded and frayed, in mohawks and buzz-cuts and scalps clean as Sinead's. All the ways of conforming to the non-conformed are here, too many to enumerate; we leave one group to join another; there's no true way to protest, only acquiesce.

Someone joins Liz. He's at an adjacent table, and he sidles over. He's blond and slick, his hair moussed up, dressed in club wear: bowler shirt, white khakis (blinding white), with spiffy leather shoes the color of horse hide. He's so very city, he sparkles, but a shine with grit. He's sharkish, and I pray my order will come sooner. I need to get.

I can hear him talking.

"Hi, sweets. Long time," he says.

"Not now," she says. "I'm with somebody."

Me, I think. Me.

"That doesn't bother me, sweets," he says. What're you doing after?"

And I can tell she doesn't want him, her fingers starting to claw at the table corner.

"Going home with him," she says, and I can tell that green-eyed glow is a look of love, not an ask for help. She can handle herself.

"Is that right?" he says.

And my order comes, and I am upon him.

I try to look suave, but look pissed, and Liz blurts, "James, this is John. He's—"

"An old friend," he says. "So old I can't wait to catch up," he says, and, "Let's go." And he takes Liz by the wrist and stands.

And she says, "John, I'm with him. With Jamie here."

"This little guy," he says. "Is that right? Come on, let's go."

"Hey," I say. "I'm right here," and I let my hands go slack and go to fists at my side and writhe, like snakes, and say, "She's with me," and at that Liz starts to brighten like a new star, like a comet coming in, circling the sun, a trail, a halo, a gold-white glow.

"Is that right?" he says. "Well, good luck, bud. She's full of fire." He turns, says, "I'll call ya later."

"No phone," she says.

"Then, I'll stop by."

And he leaves shuffling, but with spunk, like a pimp ditching a prostitute, like a gambler leaving a table.

"Who was that?" I say, not too loud, not too soft.

"A guy," she says. "Sorry." Her face darkens. She thinks. "You don't want to know."

A past plays over her eyes, like watching a too-fast movie, a hipped-up ad where 10 images flash past a second, or twenty. Too many.

I sip my coffee. She chugs hers, looking into the lights of the night. No neon here.

On our way to Grinder's, an old man in Army green, frayed, soused, holds out an arm, a hand, and I dig in my khakis for coins, but that's not what he wants.

"Hey there, sweets," he says. "Got any sugar for me."

And Liz turns again, clamps down on my hand. Another time.

"Not tonight," she says.

"Oh, come on," he says. "I'm lonely."

"I'm on a date."

"Him?" he says. "How about later?"

And we swift into the night, like a fall leaf, but it's summer, and everyone knows that, including that man on the sidewalk and the green leaves and the sun and the birds that chirp as if there's only night, and nightsong, and the sun may never set or come or shine as brightly as it does somewhere, China, this time of night.

Grinder's is not far, an old two-story with black and red bricks, sooted in an earlier era. With lots of windows all painted black, Grinder's is a hipster hangout, a place for neo-Beats to spread the tobacco incense of another era.

Stickers litter the entrance window. Bands. Yoga. Forearm Shivers and Green Day and Sister May Ignatius and Tramp Stamp and Ruskabank and so many no-name garage dreams gone down, gone under, gone into cubicle veal fattening pens, into silence and elevator muzak, where the music goes, in one ear and out into the skyscrapers that claim us, call us home, our fingers gone to keyboards, our chops silent, dry. We play then only for the Man and his concrete and steel, while the nights are held by teens full of dreams and noise. Protest is staged by those who can still hold their piss.

Before we get in the door, I say, "What's with all the guys we pass?" And I can tell Liz just wants to go in, forget. "They all seem to know you, want you," I say.

And Liz says, "I know a lot of guys."

"Seems so."

"I told you before, I heal guys. Down and out guys. Artist guys. Johns with no luck. If I were a guy, they'd call me a stud, a savior, prince."

"Stud?"

"But since I'm a gal, they call me a slut."

"I don't. Wouldn't."

"Because you're beginning to see. You're new."

"New?"

"New to the world. New to the city, this city. Welcome, Jamie! This is it."

"Are you sure?"

"It's always been this way. You just couldn't see."

"See what?"

"Life. The city. Men and women," she says and tugs my hand. "Come on. Let's go in."

The show's already in swing, a young woman in red Cons and torn jeans, some of the holes safety pinned, the slats across her jeans like shark gills, like tears that will never heal. She shouts, her voice baritone-thick, her head up, nose skyward; she's unafraid, like a madwoman in a padded room. The men howl and hoot, and the women chirp and call.

"I'm psychotic, I'm neurotic," she shouts. "I'm enticing, I'm erotic."

A retarded man in his 50s sits in a chair near the stage so he can see, hear. His body rocks with her words, his hands in his lap. He drools, he jacks, he slaps his bald head.

"Yeah, yeah, yeah," he rocks and says.

"I'm hot, I'm on fire," she says. "Come burn on me. Blaze high, blaze higher."

And slowman rocks, his eyes open, dish-like, moon-like, spotlight-like. What he wants is her, her words. Her voice, siren-like, is what he wants, that passion. She's a goddess, a priestess now, this girl in the spot, this young woman who stomps in red shoes on the peanut-shell strewn floor, beer puddling near the bar. Fascination with the abomination calls, has all our ears. All the men in the room see only her, red-shoed priestess. It does not matter what she says, just how she says it, calls.

And when she saunters off, the bar in front of her crowding with frost-topped beers, she knows she's adored, knows she's wanted. No one wants her like this during the workday week. This is where she belongs. There's no slam school in this town, no team, no group of reciters, but with her words one is forming, a troop of troubadours, a pack of poets who sing and shout their songs, their cantos, their hearts and crotches flaming the darkness, fire in the city, holy spoken flame, tongues and fiery pillars above their top notches, heads.

Slowman starts jacking, ink-like spots staining his crotch. He stands, wobbles off. Somewhere in the night, his hand pistons to his shorts, in some back parking lot, against some car window or under some lamplight. No one notices. The seed of the city is upon him, the voice of goodness, of peace, like Valkyries red-Con-girl's words ricochet and echo between gray matter and skull. With passion, her words soothe slowman into bliss, into sleep.

Inside, Liz saunters to the stage and writes her name on the open mic list. She turns to me, says, "You a poet? You a writer? Show it."

"Show what?" I say.

"Your head, heart, soul." This is more than a dare; it's a covenant.

"More like my guts, intestines," I joke. I rifle my bag and pockets for paper scraps, for poems. No dice. I say, "I didn't bring anything."

"You brought me," she says. "Brought yourself. Brought your guts. It's time to show."

"I like to read out with a page in my hand," I say, "not make it up on the spot."

"So, there's more to learn," she says. "You can learn. Now."

"What if I flop?"

"There are other guys." She turns. "I can find other guys." She smiles, a demon smirk. "I'm putting you on the list, Jamie. Good luck."

"Next up, Liz O'Malley. Let's put our hands together for little redhot Liz."

"I've got a new boy. I brought him."

Claps and whistles come from the crowd. There're hipster men,

in all black leather and black jeans and turtlenecks and black sweaters
and black button-ups, and there are office guy princes who wish they'd
stayed in soot-colored brick instead of offices down and around Union
Station, and they have on khakis and slick-sheened slacks with black
jackets or sports coats that are drabber and more matte than their office
wear, and they wear v-neck tees instead of the crew tees they wear
during the workaday at the office with starched whites and ties, and
they all clap and watch, and I can tell they know, they have heard "little
red" before, and they hold lust in their mouths and in their throats,
and lower, dollar-roll bulges, and they wait for what she has to say as
one might wait for a schoolmarm or a leather-woman with spurs and
a riding whip or a woman in all white frocks who holds court over a
white brick institution for the mad, bughouse. They listen, they wait.
What she has to say is like Hillsong angel-voice, from hymnal to the
straight-laced, the squares they once were before they descended into
this city from the suburbs. No true jobs there, in the gated places.
Only the city keeps the grip of greenbacks for those who rise on city
thermals, for those who turn cubicles into corner offices—with wit,
with endurance, through late nights and late days and pen scratch and
computer peck and all those things the ivy leaguers learn, more time
spent in office than in the apartment, more time spent praying for
dollars. What they all want now is a piece of that past they never had,
a piece of city, a little piece of skyscraper-hipster ingénue, little piece of
Liz.

After the claps, Liz says, "Jamie, Jamie, Jamie, this one's for you—
and for all you boys out there, you city princes."

She spins like a dancer at the mic, then begins.

"Calling all cocks," she says. "Calling lost cocks, all."

And the black-suited princes hoot. They raise their lit lighters.
They raise their three-quarter-full beers, the froth gone, only suds
along the glass, foam and glass kiss. They arch, they stumble, they
jostle their Gold's Gym biceps in a wave of rumble, like men at a
party where women get naked on a stage for their money.

"The muscle-head takes as much pride in his cock as in his
arms, flexing," Liz says, her voice loud and warm, as if beer-driven,
as if amber gold tempers her song, though we have not yet hit drink.

Whiskey-tempered, on she goes, like Janis Joplin, she croons, she shouts. I start to squirm. I don't know how to take it, how she talks. I've never known a woman like her, and I don't want to blend into the reptile flurry of the men in black, the princes, though I have more in common with their pasts, their neighborhoods, than her. Their aspirations and addresses were once mine.

A prince tough guy flexes his arms, his black leather jacket creaking, lizard-like.

"You can feel mine anytime, sweetie," he says. And he doesn't grin, but holds his mouth a little open.

"It's ok, hon," says Liz. "It's ok to feel your own."

Tough guy guffaws.

"The Dilbert gives rise to his dick quick as the pen click, the elevator, full of girls and perfume, going up," calls Liz.

Hipster princes click their pens. Slowman returns and rocks his chair.

"There you go," says Liz. "Click, click, click."

Some men take the pens from their jackets, from their front pockets, and click. Like bursting a Zippo into a light and waving the flame, they're hers. What she says is their command.

"A guy at the bus stop says my breasts are like cupcakes," Liz says, and the men lean in. "'How so?' I say, and he says, 'They're so small and so sweet,' he says. And I say, 'Don't you even think of trying to taste them. I don't come topped with frosting,'" she says, and I know I don't know much about her, this Liz, this girl, this young woman, and I'm not shocked, but something I cannot say.

Laughs come from the crowd. They shuffle. They adjust.

"Calling all cocks," Liz says, shouts. "Lost cocks. Calling, calling," she says. Done, she jumps, then saunters from the spot, from the stage.

And she's beside me, and an announcer in blue beret says, "Rock on, little Liz. Rock on. Next up, the object of Little Liz's affection, newbie James Keller. Let's put our hands together for lover-boy."

The men in black clap blankly, golf claps, half-hearted full-hand claps. What they want is Liz, not some little man.

"When I was little," I say. "11, 12, 14, I was a kid magician."

Yawns. Slowman stops rocking.

"My sister was my assistant," I say. "And we did an act with a rabbit. We kept rabbits out back in a hutch."

A man in black yawns a deep "who cares" yawn, pistons his hand above his crotch, a long George-Carlin jack.

"I'd light a fire," I say, "in a silver bowl, slam down the lid, and two rabbits would appear."

A man in black makes a "presto!" motion. Slowman looks like he's about to fall into sleep.

"And these little kids would crowd around, and they'd pet as applause, their hands all over fur."

And I bow, glad it's over, and I step from the stage to mild, golf-clap applause.

"And there you have it," says the emcee. "First time. We'll break now. But back in ten we'll begin with Rye Bread Riley. You won't want to miss him. His jokes are all fully toasted."

"Not bad, lover-boy," says Liz. "But let's work on your energy."

"You mean passion, grit?"

"Yes. Those two. Lots."

And we're hand in hand again in the night, sidestepping past men in Army greens seated on the sidewalk and dapper johns in city wear, men in their forties, and then men in suits, Armanis, whose fingers look like they're made to hold glass stems. So many of them call to Liz. She looks, but walks on, with me.

"You've seen one of my haunts," says Liz. "Now let's see where you're from," she says.

"I lived in Twin Oaks. Now I'm back at home with my folks."

"Not where you live. Your bed, your pad. Where you're from. Joh-Coh. Show me."

"Ok. It's not glamorous, not as ritzy as you might think. But let's go."

And we're in my car, blue Blazer with the white stripe, stolen once in the city because it's easy to steal, the Mustang auctioned before I left suburbia for the city, the beautiful women in glitzy bikinis holding big paperboard signs like the women in boxing match rings, high stepping in high heels, their hair long like Rapunzel's, their faces painted and blushed, their eyes like those of wolverines, fierce, caught holding onto something like dense, broken, burnt-out stars. My mother says, "These men on bikes, on Harleys, you see how they appreciate their women?" I say, "Worship them?" She says, "I'd like to be treated like that, like them," and I say, "You could," and she says, "Not with your father. He wants me, but doesn't worship me," and I know their marriage will never end, like energy, like God, like water, never-ending, but in this case unchanging, and I worry for her, and I pray for her, and I think of what she must have been like once, a beauty in her band uniform marching the white lines of the football field, flute in the crook of her arm, her fingers across chrome, across silver, and her notes, like birdsong, like bird chirp, like the whistles some men make for women they see walk across sidewalk beside rebar stakes, up like cattails at the jobsite, and how they appreciate beauty is crass and dirty and city as run-off water, brown and dark and oily, nothing to emulate, but what lust they have they sing, they call, as if singing for those long locks the women with boxing ring signs sport, like horsehair, like horsetails, fanned by the wind, above rump, above the muscular haunches those pretty jogging goddesses shimmy and pump as they run. We all wish we could be horses, when most of us are slower, are simpler, and are more predator than prey, but mild ones, eyes in the front, but with fangs long gone, replaced with teeth more made for munching greens and nuts.

"Shawnee Mission Parkway," Liz says. "Take us to Shawnee."

"All roads lead to Shawnee," I say." KC's oldest suburb."

"All yellow roads lead to your home," she says.

Old home," I say. "Let's click up those heels, Dorothy."

"I'm a Missouri girl," she says. "Dorothy's got nothing on me."

"She sure doesn't. She can't have all your fire."

"You know it, Jamie. One day—one night—I might just let you touch it, my fire."

And she touches my thigh, and I speed up.

We're speeding through Mission, past the little bookstore with the blue flag-like sign out front with a blue bird on the sign corner; past the last gas station before we're in Merriam, the gas station that used to use pump attendants and still have little concrete benches for these men to sit; past the Mission Mall on our right, all sparkles of yellow and white lights coming from the stacked parking lots, like a second sun; past the hospitals and dentist offices on Nall & Roe; then deeper into Shawnee Mission with its drive-thrus: Steak 'n Shake, Winstead's, Fuddruckers. The cars drift by, a smear of reds and whites, lights. I look at Liz, and she's grinning, her face so pale in streetlamp light her freckles glow. She rolls down the window, smokes. She ashes into traffic, sparkler-like splashes dropping onto blacktop; the red embers spin like dust devils in car-wheel wind, and then I see them, another set of lights. Red, white, and blue blasting, and that chirp-chirp siren bleep. A police cruiser edges us into the slow lane, the car all white with a navy stripe, which shimmers, newly waxed.

"Shit," I say.

"Got you all worked up," Liz says. "Didn't I?"

She runs a hand down my thigh, then pulls away, runs that hand through her red hair and laughs.

I'm sweating. I roll down the window, dig in my front left pocket for my wallet. *Where's my driver's license? Yes, there it is.* I search for my insurance card. *Should I go for my title in the glove box by Liz's lap?* I do. The cop's slow. It doesn't look like he'll shoot me for hunting through my car.

And then he's on us, then he's there.

"License and registration?" he says. He's about my age, blonde and buzz-cut. He's clean shaven, soft as a Dove bar. His blue eyes show like butane flames, but low-lit, calm, just blazing, not burning. And I'm not sure what to say, what to do. I give him what he wants, and he looks at the papers, thumbs my driver's license like a magician spins a card, studying, but bored with what is in his hands.

Liz jokes, "I got him all excited, sir. Second date."

And he grins, a cop smile, like he knows all the dirt we hold, and this time that means not much. This time, we're precious. He tips his hat.

"Is that right, ma'am?" he says. He winks.

"Utterly true, sir," she says.

The young policeman looks long down the road, as if the future can be seen, then looks behind him, as if his car waits like a dog for him, wanting more, wanting walked. We're nothing, an inconvenience, a bit of litter in the road.

"I'm going to let you off with a warning," he says. "But pay attention to the road. And to the speed limit. Keep it down."

He gives me back my license and papers. He looks again at Liz, and she smiles back, fetchingly.

"Thank you, sir," Liz says. Then turns to me, says, "Now hands to yourself."

I slump at the wheel, count as the cop walks, clop-clop, to his car. I wait for the police lights to go out, like a porch light extinguishing at night, signaling all's clear, now we can sleep. *Should I oull out now or wait for him to pull away and pass?* I wait. His car goes, slow, then speeds up and zooms down Shawnee Mission Parkway, like he's got somewhere to be, somewhere to go, quick-like. I've seen speed walkers with that pace, that push. He has it. Yuppies and cops, like Alice's harried white rabbit with gold pocket watch in hand, they always have somewhere to rush.

Liz says, "Jamie, you really need to learn how to talk to cops."

"How?"

"Start by talking. And apologize. Give a reason."

"Reason for what?" I say, defeated. I look to the moon.

"For breaking the law."

"Why?"

"We all need a reason," she says.

In the park darkness in the grass on 72nd Street, I slip Liz's shirt off. I fish at her bra clasp, and she says, "careful," and I slow down, study, concentrate, like a man disarming a bomb, and the latch snaps off with a twist, and my hands are on her breasts, which are cool in my hands and in the night air, and she's kissing me, and her hands are across my chest, moving from the pecs to that trace of hair, a line down my sternum to my navel and beneath, and she says, "Say something."

And I say, "It's hot on the desert plains, and the gazelles are running."

"There are no gazelles in Kansas, trigger," she says. "Especially not in Shawnee Mission."

But she gets my game, and I continue, "But I've seen some fairly close. At the Kansas City zoo. You don't live far from there."

"Yeah, right," she says. "I call it my second home."

And we've found our own language. And her hands and my hands meet, a string of laced fingers in the air, her smile like none I've ever seen. And I hear a click, and a cone of white light spreads towards us like surf. The wave of light is a police spotlight. A police car's parked perpendicular behind ours in the lot. We stand. Somehow Liz has her shirt back on. They ask us to move on, and we traipse to my car. It's almost silly, being stopped twice. Back in traffic, Liz giggles. She toys with me, her hand on my thigh.

"Careful," I say.

"Oh, you're getting used to it," she says. "Being stopped. A real city kid now."

"I try."

"Keep at it. Soon you'll be able to walk away with little guilt. One day, none."

"Show me somewhere else, somewhere quiet," she says.

"How about my high school?" I say.

"That'll do." Then she pauses, riffs, "The childhood home of young James Keller."

We're wrapped in kisses under the football field bleachers, the only light parking lot lamps up the hill. I struggle to get Liz's shirt off. Maybe I'm tiring.

"Your first time here?" she says.

"Hardly."

She says, "You sure you can get my shirt off? There's not much light."

Her shirt comes off, and I say, "Who needs light?" And a cone of light snaps on, a man in blue in the shadows.

"Game's over, folks," he says. "Move on."

And we do.

The car seems colder, as we return. Everything seems darker, as if lit by shadows. But Liz takes my hand in her hand, and she kisses my knuckles.

"Better luck next time. Better luck later," she says. "Don't give up, trigger. You know how it is."

"A cop on every corner," I say. "Stopping love at every intersection."

"You live in a loveless world," she says. "But a shiny one."

"Shiny and brightly lit."

"Repression is bright and stark and clean," she says.

"What crime is it kissing?" I say.

"Kissing just must not be right in Joh-Coh, not right for squares."

"Only in the bedroom, rings on your fingers?" I say.

She runs her hand along my fingers. No rings there. Her hands have a few, the sparkly type one finds at pawn shops, all glitter but not much worth. I remember them from when we were in the light. Now, driving, I just feel their ridges as she inspects my hands.

"You have long thin fingers," she says. "An artist's hands."

"Thanks," I say. "There's a story in that."

"Tell it."

"My father's people lived in a valley near where gypsies camped in West Bohemia," I say. "Story is the gypsies liked my people, had interest in those hands, saw us of good artist stock. The tent people started stealing the Keller children, so the Keller line picked up, carted to Russia, moved on."

"All because of fingers."

"That and starvation. Those were tough times." We pause in the night, in the lamp light, within history. "What now?" I say. "Where to?"

"My town?"

"Deal, missy. Let's get the hell out of Dodge."

"Or Joh-Coh," she says.

When we arrive, it's nearly midnight. The stars are all out strong, pin-pricks with halo swirls all around. Liz's hair is like that, like a red halo or mane, like a fire drawing notice to her pale face. She musses her hair, puts a hand on my shoulder, when I park in one of the four spots along the top of Suicide Hill, as it's called, place where youth come to end it, but we're here to begin, here in this acre-wide expanse of grass nestled in the city, which rolls east to west, high point to low. This grass patch is one big hill with a metal slide on its top, like a lookout tower. And that slide is where Liz is headed in a rush, a wild rush. She kisses my cheek and says, "Preppy, welcome to my backyard." And off goes her shirt, over her head. She makes her way out of her jeans as walks toward the slide. Now only in her bra and bottoms, all pink and lace, she scales the metal slide steps, sometimes taking two at a time, and I say, "Nice backyard," and I take off my shirt, follow. Slower, but I follow. What have I gotten into? And Liz says, "Preppy, you look better without your shirt."

"But I'm uneven," I say, pointing to my pecs.

"Like Jim Morrison, honey," she says. "One pec's a little off. I like it," she says. "My little Lizard King." And she slides down, all skin and lace and sweat and city mist. Am I imagining this, in some dream? She curls a finger at me.

"Come on, baby, light my fire," she says.

I approach her, and straddled at the bottom of the slide, she grasps my middle and slips my belt off. A small black plastic film canister slips from my front pocket and thumps on the slide.

"What's this?" she says. "You a photographer?" She opens the canister. "Wanna take some sexy pictures of me?" she says. And a condom falls from the canister into her hand. "Sly devil," she says. "What's this?"

"Reinforcements."

"Ever used one?"

"Not yet."

"Ok, preppy. Not here. Not now. But sometime. Some place proper."

"Proper?"

"Proper, preppy. Proper."

She leans and kisses me deeply, and I wonder if my quest for experience, carnal and exploratory, has begun. I wonder if this Beat world is the one I've always been looking for and now it's come, here in the city, with this beautiful girl at the base of the slide at Suicide Hill. Into that kiss I go.

Later, we're on the sidewalk again, clothed, hand in hand. We swing that fist our hands make, laced.

"I think I want you to stay over tonight," Liz says. "But first: Jack and Coke."

"Jack and Coke? Friends of yours?" I say.

"Old friends. Let's pick up my friends and drink. See how far we get."

"How far do you think?" I say.

"Don't be dense."

"You don't keep drinks ready? At home?"

"I'm 19, preppy. Can't. To Gomer's Liquor!"

Gomer's is a long, squat, white block building, humble with blacked out windows. The white block is tarnished, sooted, and marked by hands run along the walls. The sidewalk is crumbled and cracked along the store. Decades have passed, but the building is the same, small, a bunker in a city grown up around its white walls. The streetlamps are weak here. Though not dangerous, it's dark.

Liz takes my hand and leads me in. The store doors swish behind us when we enter. There is so much to look at, all of the colors, the labels, the shapes and sizes of the bottles. I gawk. Liz picks a big bottle of Jack Daniels from the shelf and presses the bottle into my chest, and I take hold. Then she hooks a bottle of Coke and leads me by the hand to the cashier, a thin, grey, goateed man.

"That all, kids?" he says.

"Kids!" Liz says.

I pull forth my wallet and display my driver's license, taken against blue, my hair a little shorter, my glasses half as strong. I was pinker then and more cleanly shorn.

"You are," he says to Liz, and to me, "He just passes."

"Tie goes to the runner," I say.

"Close one," says the cashier.

Liz is shaking, incensed. She pulls hard on my hand, once we're out the door.

"Some nerve," she says.

"Don't worry," I say. "We'll grow."

"You will," she says, suggestively, and she kisses me.

On our way, we pass Jimmy's Jigger, attached to Jazz. We come upon an empty beer bottle, a brown one, diagonal to our path. It seems to want to spin there. But Liz has another notion. She stops and listens to the young men in sports jackets, sitting on the patio, with shoes worth more than two weeks of their waitress' work. She says, "Listen to them," and I do. They banter like businessmen imitating gangstas. "Yeah, you got that right, dawg. I got your back, and I know the way back to her apartment, too." Somewhere in the air is the smell of crisp, new bills, and then we see them, fanned, in front of them. They parse out a few and pay and tip the waitress. "This," Liz says, "is what I hate."

"What?" I say.

She says, "Them." And she lifts the neck of the bottle with her toes, bends her knee as a punter might, and flicks the bottle into the crowd of promising young men on the patio, who now are lighting a round of cigars. The bottle lifts and flies above them. No one notices, until it comes down and lets loose a light rain of shattered glass along the surface of the patio concrete. Some men spill drinks on themselves.

Others lose the light in their cigars. There is some shouting, while Liz raises her head, points her nose upwards, and marches on, with me trailing after her. "Rich fucks!" she says. We walk the long blocks back into her smaller, darker part of the city.

In Liz's room, lit by yellow candle light, Liz starts in, "Those guys are fucked. Full of cash and lust, spit." She spits on the floor, wipes her lips.

"Entitlement," I say.

"Yes. Fuckin' money-heaped. White boys."

I hold out my arm, "But we're white."

"Not like that," she says. "Not white gold."

Liz twists off the Jack Daniel's cap. She pours me a red plastic cup.

"To not being white gold," I say.

Liz and I clink cups, a plastic thump.

"Rich fucks," says Liz.

I suddenly notice the time, the night coming on, how everything seems to stretch. This moment takes up so much space, like it'll never end. Like the moment burnt bright, like a star exploding, the star dust blossoming outward for centuries.

I check my watch, the chain stretching from my belt loop, the gold pocket watch my father's father gave him, a railroad watch, simple, classy.

"You have somewhere else to be?" Liz says. "Someone else to see?"

"No," I say. "I just like to know the time."

"It's now. The time is now."

She kisses me.

"Forget everything else," she says. And she palms my watch and filches the chain from my belt. She steps to the window and tosses the watch out.

I look into the night, how dark it is. How will I ever find my watch?

"What the fuck!"

"Be with me or be without me," she says. "But don't check your goddamned watch."

My shoulders fall. "With you," I say. "I'll be with you." I kiss her.

When I wake, the room is yellow with morning light. The window still open, the air holds flower pollen, a tinge of exhaust, and the tang of freshly mown grass.

Liz sprawls naked on the mattress beside me, not much of the covers on. She seems so pale, as if she is always depicted in black and white, her skin the shade of fine photographic paper, Ilford fiber. I want to touch her, but I don't want to wake her, and I want to watch her breathe, like light wind going over the petals of white iris. Her life held in such beauty and fragility and strength.

I look down. I'm in my tighty whiteys. I pull at the elastic, look down. Liz awakens, stretches a long, thin, strawberry-freckled arm.

"Did we?" I say.

"No," she says. It's as if I'd told a childish joke.

"Why?"

"You were too drunk to do it proper," she says. "Another time."

I look to the window, to all of that yellow light.

"Fuck. It's morning."

"What's fucked about that," she says.

"My parents. I didn't call. Didn't go home."

I go to check my watch, but think better of it. I look to the window. Rush to the sill and look out. Nothing glints gold, just rows of orange iris wave in wind, tousle their bonnets, wag their stamen tongues, like quiet bells ringing.

"They'll live," says Liz.

"Can I use your phone?"

"You mean my parents' phone," she says.

"Yeah."

"Downstairs. By the kitchen. It's red."

She pecks me on the cheek, a morning kiss. She's digging this, me squirming, me caught in the net of the bourgeois.

"Thanks," I say and throw on some clothes. I make for the door, but notice the padlock holding us in, locked.

"Do I need a combo to get out?"

"We all do," she says.

"The numbers?"

"3-11-24," she says.

I turn the lock dial, "3. 11. 24."

The lock pops open, and I pull it from its loop and long harness.

"Got it," I say. "Back in a sec."

"Tell Mommy and Daddy hi from me," she says and flips her wrist, debutante-like.

"Sure."

I rush from the room and down the old wooden stairs, my bare feet slapping as I go.

No one around, I slump against a yellowed dining room wall, the wall smoke-stained, smudgy. The red phone cord stretches as far as it can, coming from the kitchen, the red curls all taut, pulled. I know how I must look: beat, repentant, worried, deep-hewn furrows in my brow, plowed.

"Mom," I say. "It's me."

"You ok? Where are you?"

"I'm at Liz's," I say. "I stayed the night."

"Why didn't you call?" She sounds tired, on edge.

"I lost track of time."

"You know, I've been sitting here on the couch all night in my housecoat, my sneakers on, ready to come help haul you out of some ditch. Did you think of that?"

"No. I'm sorry, Mom."

"Why didn't you just come home?"

"I'd been drinking a little. Didn't think it'd be safe." I pull the tab off a beer can tipped and tilted against the wall.

"Drinking?" she said. "I could've come got you. You should have called."

"Sorry. I'm sorry, Mom," I say. "I'll come home now."

"We need to talk. Your being with this girl, Liz, is becoming a liability."

"Liability?"

"Just come home."

My mother is seated on a rusted metal deck chair, high above the neighborhood, when I arrive. Though rusted below, new summer cushions are fitted and tied to the chairs, a wash of muted blues and cream, something from Target or Pier One. My mother's still in her housecoat and red sneakers. Her hair is wild in the wind. She hasn't showered.

I climb the redwood steps to greet her, steps that creak with my footfalls. We built this deck together when I was 12. My father, a carpenter, takes pride in it, what he has made. I was a go-fer. Father taught me to sink a nail in two hits, like him, but it still takes me five or seven taps to get a ten-penny nail sunk in.

Mother motions for me to sit, and I do. She's unhappy, her face a twist of worry.

"I'm disappointed in you, son. And worried."

"I'm sorry," I say. "I should have called."

"It's not that. It's her."

"What about her?" I say.

"I think she's wild. Steering you down a dark road," and she waves her hand as if the air around is one dark winding road, an orbit of bad luck and folly.

"She's just vibrant," I say. "Alive. Full of pluck."

"Full of what?"

"Pluck. With a *p*"

"I thought you said something else."

"What, *fuck*?" I say.

"I didn't raise you to talk like that."

"It's just a word for a thing people in love do." And I wonder how often my mother and father have sex. I look. I wait.

"You're too young to be in love like that."

"I'm 21. I can die for my country. I can drink."

"I hope you don't do either."

"Come on, Mom."

"I think this girl of yours is a bad influence, a liability, a bad seed."

"She's just *city*, Mom."

"I didn't raise you to like the city."

"But I do. It's where jazz is, jazz lives," and I see the coffee shops and clubs I love in my mind: the brick, the blue neon light, the glasses and saucers full of fizz and steam.

"You get that *city* girl pregnant, and she'll have to come to love the suburbs."

"Mom!"

"You know what I mean."

And my mother strides inside, the long white ties from her housecoat trailing. She opens the glass deck door and lets the door fall behind her, a swish and a metallic slam. She doesn't look back.

That night, the city lights around us like blurred Christmas bulbs, I kiss Liz with renewed passion, abandon. Here in the indigo night, the stars a-swirl, I lean in. I pull Liz to me. I kiss her as if this might be our first or last kiss. That sort.

"Stop that," she says.

"Stop what?"

"That kid attempt at a French kiss." Her lip curls. She's pissed.

"French?"

"Baby," she says. "You're sure not French."

"I know. I know."

"Just go on and kiss me in your own small, suburban, repressed way. I don't mind," she says. "I don't mind that much."

I try not to sulk as we walk the blacktop and the sidewalk hand in hand. Liz lifts and lofts our hands, and it's almost like we're skipping along in a scene to The Wizard of Oz. She's in love with life, even when I'm down, in gray clouds, even when my kisses only irk her.

We pass a tall man in white collar and blue jeans, the bottoms of his jeans cuffs frayed, a wash out, as if he's someone who used to dress neat, but has fallen on tough times. His red hair is buzz cut on top and strewn in a mullet behind. He's got expensive glasses on, duct-taped at one hinge. He spits when we approach.

"Hey, baby," he says. "What you doin'?" He pulls a toothpick from his front pocket and twists the stick in his mouth.

"Nothing doin'. Can't you see I'm with him?" says Liz.

"For now."

"Back off," she says.

"Later."

"You wish," she says.

"I know, baby," he says. "I don't think."

Liz spits back and flips him off, her bird finger high and red and taut, like a stick or prick.

"Ok, baby," he says. "Fuck you, too."

Liz knows lots of men. I wonder if I'll end up in a fight over her or if I'll be left behind like that guy, our bird fingers in the air. But for now, we're hand in hand, and she's smiling again, and then her face goes placid, goes smooth, goes serious as polished stone.

"Preppy, hon. I've got something to tell you."

"Ok," I say.

"Something hard," she says.

"Shoot."

"I was with him the other night."

"Who?"

"That guy."

"Bird guy?"

"Yep. Bird guy."

I look down at my shoes, dark Doc Martin's with lots of sidewalk scuffs. There's no augury there, no sign. I look into Liz's jade eyes. I look away, into the city.

"Why?"

"I like to fuck men," she says. "I like to fuck. Can't help it. It's my thing."

"Your thing?"

"Yep. It's what I do. What I do best."

"What about me?"

"You're not ready yet," she says.

"Why not?"

"I want to do it right," she says.

"When?"

"When it's time. You ok with that?" she says.

"I guess I gotta be."

"You're sweet," she says, touching my cheek. "Sweet, sweet, baby James."

"How should I think about this, about us?"

"You're mine," she says. "I might stray a bit, but you're mine."

"What now?" I look at her, then past her, into the city: the lights, the shadows and silhouettes, like walking into an Aaron Douglas painting, everything has an edge, no colors blend. The colors and shadows just stop, each thing distinct, but with so so much going on, the bustle of the hive of humanity: the hip city kids that bounce in their red high tops when they walk, a basketball tucked under one arm; the business ladies with their click-click heels, their faces upturned, their pink purses clutched, huffed; the business guys that slink by, chests up, legs long, their black slacks swishing when they stride.

"Let's dance," she says.

"Now step forward with your left foot with authority," says Liz. "Move me." We're in EE's Dance, a long low building of polished black granite-like stone. It's upscale with a large long bay window along the street side, something for passersby to peer in as they stroll this brightly lit block. Streetlamps seem to shine down every few steps of the sidewalk.

Liz has my hand on her back. She positions me. She takes a toe and pushes at my feet, reworking my stance.

"Like this?" I say.

"Don't ask. Do," she says.

I step forward. I do so as deliberately as I can. I imagine a bullfighter in his sequins and flowy cape, his concentrated eyes that can stop or slow a bull, his small tight energy. I want to be like him.

"Not bad," she says. "Right foot now. Same thing."

I step.

"Good," she says. "Let's just walk this way now. Walk me back."

And I walk like marching, but with more grace, with the bullfighter's sure steps or the male ballet dancer with his telltale bulge.

"Left, right. Left, right. Walk me back across the floor," she says.

And I'm dancing, I'm walking, I'm strutting. I've never danced this way. Whatever it is, this seems to thrill Liz, teaching me. She's serious, her face polished rock, but there's a light in her eyes, as if she's watching orange campfire embers rise in wind, as if she sees a future in us, in my feet.

Soon, we're back hand in hand on the walk, out of the white-lit EE's side of the city and passing a line of concert-goers queued outside the yellow-bulb Grand Emporia, yellow o's and red neon, the marquee like a temple eye in the night.

"This is my city," she says, "its gray slinky starter pants cats, its hunter green fatigue vets, its black leather miniskirt corner girls. Its madness. Its morning light with lemon rinds and condoms, spent. Its cig tips illuminating night, illuminating dawn, like searchlights, like cat eyes, like firefly butts, signaling: come on, come on, follow me. Follow."

The light over Liz's front door shines like a lantern light, bright but low, dull, casting just enough shine to illuminate the door and the first step. Liz grins.

"Home, sweet home. Follow me," she says.

"Ok."

"Follow me in."

At the kitchen table sit Liz's parents, drinking from long brown bottles, smoking from bright white cigarettes. The room is awash with color and grit, what a party looks like when you're older and settled, what the end of a workaday sinks and pools into.

Liz's mother, about 45, looks tired, her hair beautiful and long, red, but darker than Liz's, and stringy. Liz's father, who appears to be a little younger, looks even more tired, his face gray. Both have on sweats, father with brown, sockless loafers.

"Mom, Dad, meet James," Liz says.

"How are you, son?" says Liz's father. "You were here the other night, weren't you?"

"Yes, sir."

"Sweetie," says Liz's mother, ashing as she speaks, tapping her cig tip into an overflowing tray, "our house is your house. Lizzie stayed, pays her rent. Kept her room. So, who she brings home is welcome. You're her concern." Her voice is bright, with a lilt, though tired, with a little gravel in the throat.

"Look at him," says father. "He's no concern. Nice clothes. Manners. Nice smile."

"Better than most," says mother.

"Clean. Laced up real tight," says father.

"Hey, Pops," says Liz. "I'm right here. He's not some steer for you two to appraise."

"Missy," says father, "you bring them into the barn, we're allowed to talk."

"And who is this?" Liz's sister comes down the stairs with a flourish and flounces into the kitchen as if the linoleum is a fashion show catwalk. She sweeps her light green summer dress and sits.

"Hey, little sister," Liz says. "Nice dress."

"You weren't using it."

"You're more than using it."

"Thanks."

Liz's sister extends a hand, and I shake carefully. Her hand is warm, flushed.

"Cassandra," she says. "Call me Cass."

I try not to, but I'm taken with her. I try to be placid, calm.

"Jamie, Jamie, Jamie," says Liz, shaking her head.

Cass rustles her dress like a can-can, grins. And Liz's mother and father stand.

"We should go," says father.

"Have fun," says mother.

Liz's mother and father traipse upstairs, loping hand in hand. Halfway up, father releases hands and cups mother's ass with a clap.

"Oh, Pops," says mother.

"Old goat," Liz says.

"Stallion, stud," says Cass.

Cass cuts eyes at me. She seems to see something she likes.

"This one's not bad, either, Sis," she says. "Squeaky clean fresh."

"Eyes off," says Liz.

"You're like rosewater," Cass says.

"Rosewater?" I say.

"Something sweet to put on."

Liz hooks a hand around me, her arm constricting around my shoulders, neck.

"Mine, mine, mine," says Liz.

Cass says, "Let the man decide."

"Sorry," I say. "I'm with her."

"*Little* Sis," says Liz.

"Suit yourself," says Cass, and Cass crosses and uncrosses her legs, leans in. Her fingers are near mine on the table.

"Get off," says Liz.

"What do you do?" says Cass. She leans a little in.

"I read poetry to old folks."

"Artist, poet. Just like Sis. My type," she says.

"Mine," says Liz.

Cass touches a finger to my wrist, says, "Opposites attract." She points to me: "Artist," then to herself: "Model." She says, "Liz is just like you. Too much like you."

Liz stomps off, her hair like fire. She flips open the front door and shoots out, leaving the big wooden door, with all of its amber and tarnished locks, gaping behind her. In come the city sounds, the traffic waves and hum, the radios pumped up too loud.

"You'd better get her," says Cass. "She's fire. Has been since she took too much acid and got addicted to Mini Thins: cheap, legal speed. Her emotions are whacked."

"Sure it's not the competition?" I say.

"Just playin'."

When I go out, I close the door behind me, the latches clicking into place, the door making a shoosh sound when wood and metal meet. Too careful, I think. I'm slow coming, not knowing what I'll see. Liz is in the front yard, her back to me, one leg twitching, her arms crossed. I can see her fingers at her shoulders. She turns.

"Bye," she says.

"What?"

"Bye, bye, bye."

"What? Why?" I say.

"You want my little sister? Have her."

"But I want you," I say. I didn't want her sister. I just watched her.

"Prove it," she says.

And I step to her, French kiss her.

"You're still no good," she says.

"I try."

"Don't try. Do," she says.

I kiss her again, slower, calling her back, my lips on her lips, a taste. I pull at her lips with my lips.

"Sorry, Jamie. No dice. Bye."

"Please," I say.

Liz stomps off, headed toward her front door. "Bye, bye, bye," she says.

I march up to her.

"Get," she says.

I lie down in the yard, like resting in front of a tank.

"Can't squat here," she says. "Go! Bye."

"I'll be back tomorrow," I say, "when you cool off." I rise.

"Jamie, you never learn. There's no cooling me. Bye!"

"What's that mean, *bye*?"

"It's over," she says. "We're over. Go fuck my little sister. Bye!"

"I don't want her. I want you."

"I saw how you looked at her. How everyone looks at her. Bye!"

Liz steps to me, kisses me hard on the mouth, then kisses my neck hard, swift, pulling at me.

"Bye!"

"What? Fuck that hurt." There's got to be a blooming hickey on my neck, I know.

"Something to remember me by. Bye!"

"Please," I say.

Liz stomps off into the house and slams the door. I follow, ring the bell.

"Bye, Jamie. Go home."

At Lean's, I toggle a tank across an on-screen desert. The tank's slow in the sand, not stuck, but almost. What am I driving over and into? A heavy round hits my tank, and that metal box on treads goes up in a fiery explosion, red and yellow blasting up and a white smoke cloud follows, billowing.

"Sorry, dude," says Lean. "Wanna talk?"

"Not really."

"Suit yourself. You're up. Ready player one."

I'm at work, at the nursing home ("assisted living facility") in Olathe. Not a bad place. Upscale. No cockroaches walking across the mashed potatoes, leaving a line of footprints. No low lights, the room lit by the blue tube TV. No mice among the couch feet. But instead bright fluorescent lights, just a little blue-green in the glow. White-coated orderlies, like nurses. Nice orthopedic shoes, pushing, pulling, tugging at the arm coats of the old. *Come, come here.* The old are slow: in walkers, on canes, in wheel carts, slow-footed, zombie-walking. But some smile. Some drool, a line, like a snail's, following them down the hall and into the room where I stand with a three-ring binder in hand and a label on the front, "Poetry Lite." I took over when my mentor left town. She gave me all of her gigs. At $75 a pop, it's not that bad. I do a lot of driving, my car full of poetry anthologies—and these binders I make, full of poems I've selected for the group, some printed, some handwritten. I'm learning what they like.

"Here's one by William Carlos Williams," I say, "Spanish-American poet of the turn of the century, poet and country doctor, who wrote poems on prescription pads in between patients. Here's 'Spring and All.'"

The old squirm. Something's coming.

"'By the road to the contagious hospital—'"

"No hospital. No hospital," a woman calls. She's blue haired with a thin hair scarf wrapped around. She's got yellow, crooked teeth. She's slumped in her wheelchair, but her head is up, bird-like. She's ready to squawk and call and cuss. She rocks in her chair, just a tick-tock, pendulum rock.

I continue, "'under the surge of the blue.'"

She rocks in her chair, calls, "No hospital. No hospital." She shakes a fist, turns to others. "No hospital. No hospital."

"'Mottled clouds drive from the northeast—a cold wind,'" I say.

"No hospital. No hospital."

She squirms, she rocks, tries to launch out of her chair, a hand up, a fist.

"'Lifeless…sluggish, dazed spring approaches—they enter the world naked, cold, uncertain of all save that they enter.'"

The old woman reaches across her chair and fists some flatware from her neighbor's tray. "Hey," the other woman, her vocal chords old and dry, whispers. Old woman pitches that knife and fork and spoon at me with all she's got, and the metal trio clanks on the linoleum floor at my feet.

"That one must've hit too close to home," I joke. "I apologize."

And the young men and women in white come, quick, and wheel the old woman away, her hands up, her neck and head jerking. She wants at me. She wants me done.

The orderlies wheel in an old man in the old woman's place. The old man holds a football in his lap. The orderlies call him Coach.

I say, "This one's for coach," who is motionless, blanked out, his face: stone. He does not acknowledge my quip, my call, my honor to who he is or was.

"'Autumn Begins in Martin's Ferry, Ohio,'" I say. "By James Wright."

Others in chairs, lean in, listen.

"'In the Shreve Hill football stadium, I think of Polacks nursing long beers in Tiltonsville…'"

The crowd listens, their eyes glassy, but with light. They like this one. The crowd might be called enraptured, including coach, who moves, who moves his head, nodding to the words, listening with his face.

"'…All the proud fathers are ashamed to go home. Their women cluck like starved pullets, dying for love.'"

Two women nod. They know chickens.

"'Therefore, their sons grow suicidally beautiful at the beginning of October, and gallop terribly against each other's bodies.'"

I've touched Coach's mind, body. His face goes bright, breaking through a cloud. He wriggles in his chair in delight.

"Yes. Yes, boys," he says. "Take it inside. Throw long now. Run, boys. Run!"

An orderly takes hold of Coach's chair.

"Coach," he says. "What was that? You're back." And the orderly says to me, "Coach hasn't spoken in months."

He wheels Coach to me, and I put a hand on Coach's shoulder. I say, "'Therefore, their sons grow suicidally beautiful at the beginning of October, and gallop terribly against each other's bodies.'"

"Yes," says Coach. "Yes. Gallop. Run!"

"She gone?" my mother says.

We're back on the deck, the birds on the wire, the squirrels running the fence, the sun out as if all we're made to do is sit and watch that yellow-white dot move across the sky then set. Mother wears tall, dark sunglasses and a wicker hat. She has a flowy summer shirt, like those one would wear to the beach, and khakis, sandals. She's rested. Her hair's perfect, dark brown mocha locks up in the wind, up over her ears. She smiles and waits, like a card player with a perfect hand, royal flush or four of a kind.

"Who gone?"

"That girl. City girl," she says.

"Yes."

"You miss her, don't you?"

"Yes, Mom. I feel it here," and I point to my heart, circle my heart.

"In your heart. Affection can do that."

"Affection? Why not love?"

"Wild oats, son. That's all."

"Mom!"

"And she was kind of—how shall I say—trampy."

"She's no tramp."

"Really? How many guys do you think she's been with?"

"A few."

"Not a lot?" she says.

"Ok, maybe a lot, but a man's like that, and they call him a stud. Why's it different for women?"

"Tall trees of Georgia. You know that song?"

"No."

"Babies then. Because of babies, son. Blood goes with the mother. She takes care, while a man can just wander off."

"You seen Liz?" I say.

"Pretty redhead?" says the guy next to me at the bar at 51st Street Coffee. He's a regular. Everyone calls him "Painter." He's leather-faced, hard living. He takes a gulp of his tall beer. Wipes the creases from his brow with one tan hand.

"Yes," I say.

"Fiery gal," he says.

"Tell me about it."

"Painted her last night," he says. And Painter points to the coffee shop wall, where a big, finger-painted portrait hangs. In it, Liz is nude, her hair Medusa-like. The background sings and swims with sperm-like wrigglers, squiggles painted with the small finger. The hair and the body are painted with thicker strokes, also squiggly. There's passion there, fire in those lines.

"Really?" I say.

"Hung it this afternoon."

"She mention me?"

"No. Didn't talk about guys. Only art." He swigs some dark beer, looks around.

"Art?"

"How she wants to be seen. Last. Immortal. Typical youth wish."

"Where'd you learn to paint?"

"Prison. No brushes the day I started. Just paint. So, I used my hands. My fingers."

Later that night, I spot Archie with his wheelbarrow, a blue tarp pulled over his stuff, wheeling toward Nichol's Lunch and his mother's home. He's wading through traffic, when I first see him, moving slow, deliberately. Nothing wrong here, nothing to see. I wave, and he speeds up a little, not happy to see me or not happy to see anyone, I can't be sure.

"Archie!"

"Not talkin' to you," he says. He wheels along the sidewalk, and we walk side by side, slowly toward Nichol's Lunch with its bright, yellow sign, a beacon in the night.

"Why not?"

"You were Liz's friend, and Liz's all broken up. She's a shattered mirror over you."

"But she broke up with me."

"That doesn't matter to me, bub. How ever it happened, it broke her."

"But—"

"No buts about it, fella. She's gone."

"What? Where'd she go?"

"Parents sent her away."

"To—"

"Midwest Regional's my guess," says Archie.

"What's that?"

"Nut house, bughouse, place for little ladies who've lost their wits."

"Why?"

Archie stops his cart, the wheelbarrow in the center of the Nichol's Lunch parking lot.

"Too much trouble, I think. Little lady'd started too much shit— yelling, throwing things, slammin' doors, and stompin' 'round."

"Really? That enough?"

"Just a typical diva day, I say. But her parents…"

"She doesn't belong there," I say.

"You're telling me, compadre. Why so down?"

"Why not? My girl's been locked up."

"Let me buy you a drink."

Archie stows his things at his mother's house, then takes me for a drink at Missy B's, a few doors down from Nichol's Lunch. Over the bar, there's a graphic of two big beer mugs clinking together with a rainbow emanating from their union. A TV's on. There are rows upon rows of liquor beneath the TV, many I've never known. Lots to mix with, like Amaretto.

"This is a gay bar, isn't it?" I say.

"What other kind?" says Archie.

"What'll it be, Archie?" says the bartender. He's slim with a shaved head and handle bar mustache. His eyes are piercingly blue. He wears a bowler shirt and stone-washed jeans.

"A vodka tonic—and one for my compatriot," says Archie.

"Comin' up," and the bartender turns to me, "Why the long face, partner?"

"He lost his girl," says Archie.

"Girls! Who needs 'em," he says.

The bartender lifts a bottle and pours, pushes a button for fizz. A newscast hums from the TV, "Experts postulate that a tourist who engaged in a sexual act with an African green monkey with the AIDS virus transferred the disease commonly found in that genus to humankind."

"Probably some straight man," says the bartender, "that fucked that monkey. Too little to diddle his own kind."

"Bet so," I say.

"The straights blame us, me and my boys, when it's really all their fault," says the bartender. "This shit."

"Our fault," I say. "Sorry."

"It's ok," he says. "I don't blame you."

"That's right, Jamie," says Archie. "I know you wouldn't fuck a monkey, would you?"

"No. I haven't fucked anyone or anything."

"Somebody need to teach you?" says the bartender.

"Sister Liz was on that," says Archie. "Now she's gone."

That night, and during the days that follow, I look for Liz. I try her house. The door's locked, and the light's off. I ring. I knock. No one comes. No one's home. There's a darkness there. The lilies out front droop. I scout around among the dried, brown blooms, their petals like spent crepe paper. There's still a little green in the stems near the dirt, near the ground. The bulb's somewhere below, pushing energy up, although there's nothing much left, no hope. I push a hand around the stems, searching. I can't see much, so I let my fingers guide me in the shadows, and then I find something. My watch, the cover thrust open by the fall. I look, I shake the watch. The timepiece still counts minutes, counts seconds. The hands move as if they'd never been dropped. No scratches, no scrapes, just a little dirt along the hinge. I hold the watch up to light as if it's a sundial. My father's father's watch. I want to kiss it, but don't. I unkink the watch's linked leash and attach the metal string to my belt loop and sink the watch into my pocket once again. Something good has come.

I walk in front of the coffee shop, look in the window. There are men in black leather vests with silver studs, women with purple hair, spiked up. There are the bowler shirt guys, in their forties, wearing dress shoes with no socks, still hanging on. There are lots of types, but no Liz.

I hike up the grass to the slide at Suicide Hill. No one's around. The wind tousles the tops of the grass blades, thick bluish crabgrass, mostly. No one mows. No Liz.

I walk over the blurred rainbow-colored sidewalk poems. Only a few words can be parsed. The rest are foot-worn and rain blurred. I do the Loose Park loop, walk the whole lakefront. No Liz.

I drive downtown, park, and walk by Grinder's, look in the blacked-out window, my hand and face to the glass. No one but the bartender in. No Liz. Spent lemons and cigarettes line the curb.

I try EE's. Inside, young women waltz old men, slender young women, brunettes and blondes, and the men have monk-cuts or have lost their hair, their heads cue-bald, liver-spotted. No Liz.

I'm back on the stand where it started, behind my drums at 51st Street Coffee, with Ryan Mix's trio, with Sean on guitar instead of percussionist Billy Dee. Ryan's shaved the last wisps of his hair, gone bald. Gaunt, with a hint of the bulldog's jowls, his face shorn clean as a baby's butt, Ryan's decked out in all black: button down shirt and black slacks, black leather vest that doesn't quite fit (too tight), the vest rides up on and hugs his ribs. He's leading well tonight, pioneering us through Monk and Mingus tunes, some of which we don't know, but learn on the stand. Ryan's older than us, about 45, but he looks 55, 'cause he drinks so much, so hard, so long. So many years. Sean Cassapaglia is on guitar. He's a few years older than me, 26 or so, and we used to play together in Hester & the Jazz Puritans for popcorn before movies at The Englewood, then in Three Against One at the Nelson Food Court. Sean's thick, Italian American, anvil-chinned with a deep five o'clock shadow, and he's wild as Kerouac's Cassady, and, if I'd let him, would get me into just as much trouble, gigging and driving across town and into the surrounding towns, our gear tossed into the back of his truck. Ryan picks his Guinness beer off Sean's corduroy amp, leaving a dark brown ring on the tan fabric. We're mid-tune, Ryan sipping during Sean's guitar solo, and I think Sean's going to set down his guitar and beat Ryan with his axe, seeing that ring. "That amp's new, you MF," Sean whispers, and plays down a dark tunnel of mixolydian chords, the fifth as the root, and goes minor, goes dark, and extends ably to sevenths and ninths and thirteenths, and Ryan comps handily, a champ with chords he can also almost do Sean with one hand, and so the two meet in the middle, come to a truce through the tune, Ryan supporting Sean's dip into darkness, and I brush along, my whisks over snare drum head, spinning rings, spinning corner-chopped triangles, spinning figure eights. With these two string-slingers, sometimes it pays to play quiet, and I do, until Sean again decides to spin his volume knob and play electric the way the instrument sometimes wishes: to shout, to keen, to grate at the lining of the metal coffee shop roof. Ryan's not into that, and he quiets us down when he can, and when we take a break, after Sean's long solo, Sean's rubbing at the corduroy stain with a hanky, dipping water from his ice glass. Sean doesn't drink, at least not at gigs. Neither do I. And Ryan's gone to the men's room or his car to smoke, to toke.

When Ryan's back, and has spoken to Sean, before we kick the gig, the set, Ryan says, "Where's your girl?"

"Girl?" I say.

"Red head."

"I don't know."

"Miss her?"

"Sure do," I say.

"Well, let's find her."

"How?"

"I have ways," says Ryan. "Come with me, when we're done. Bring your drums."

Sean throws me a look, itches his chin with his middle finger: "Good luck."

When we stop, Ryan lugs his upright bass out of the car in one heave, and the bass holds to his shoulder by a black case strap. He moves like a man carrying a big bag of cash or another man, a corpse. He knows this walk, the right foot pivoting and planting hard. We're at a little house on Cherry Street, nice neighborhood, a dozen blocks from the city.

Ryan calls back to me, "Just your snare drum and brushes."

So, this will be a quiet gig. I pull my drums from the car, loaded down like a Sherpa, and I lug all the drums in one heft, one trip. When we get to the door, I ask Ryan, "What exactly are we doing here?" and Ryan says, "Serenading my ex-wife."

A woman comes to the door and greets us. She doesn't seem to be expecting the visit.

"Ryan," she says.

"Hi, love."

"Oh, you. Come in, tattered man."

Soon, we're on Anne's back porch. I learn Anne's been divorced from Ryan for about a year. She's on a lawn chair with those woven green straps for a seat. She seems to be in her 40s. She has jean shorts on, crosses her legs, and seems mildly interested in our show, but flattered. Ryan plays a bass solo intro, "So What?" that Miles Davis tune made for the bass. I brush along, try to whisper love using wire whisks on calfskin drum head. I strive to make every pattern smooth, like palming water or like grain sifting through fingers into a small pile.

"You like it, honey?" says Ryan.

"Two strapping young jazz men serenading me. How can you go wrong?

"Young?" says Ryan.

"Young enough," she says.

"We in tune?" Ryan asks.

Anne rises and touches Ryan's cheek, nonchalant as wiping

something off, and she pecks him a kiss.

"Perfectly," she says.

About an hour later, we're in Anne's living room. Anne hands me a wine bottle. The green bottle glass glints in yellow lamp light.

"Help me with this?" she says.

"I'm not very good," I say.

I twist and sink the corkscrew, pull. As if magic, the corkscrew comes out with the first long pull.

"Better than me," she says.

"Should he be drinking?" I say. Ryan drinks too much, goes on benders, I hear.

"I like him better that way," she says.

Anne and Ryan are on the couch, sipping wine. Cans and bottles litter the table, litter the floor. I'm in a folding chair, watching, not sure what to say, do. Should I go? I can't walk back. So, I watch their love, like orange campfire embers catching at brown leaves or paper, flashing back into fire.

"Look at us. Love birds again," Ryan says.

"You wish."

"Want a refill?" he says.

"On wine, on song, on everything," she says.

Ryan picks up his bass, plays a few lines, runs a finger along a string, makes it moan.

"Too drunk," he says.

He stops, his head slumped to the side.

"Baby, I like you that way," Anne says.

"I bet you do," he says.

Ryan waddles into the next room, pulling his vest and shirt off as he goes, leaving his tops on the floor in a wad, in a heap.

"Ryan's in love with my hot tub," she says. "Much as me."

"How about you two?" I say.

"We can't live together, but we can drink together. Always have."

"Beautiful," I say.

"You know, I know where your girl is. It's why Ryan brought you here."

"Where?"

"Midwest Mental Health. Parents put her in. I run the front desk."

"Oh no. I feared that'd be it."

"Yep. They got tired of her."

"I never will," I say.

"Give it time," she says. "I know you love her. Does she love you back?"

"She did."

"She might again," says Anne.

Then a premonition comes over us, like a breeze, like a wind straightening the hairs on our arms and blowing across the skin, waving our arm hairs like tan prairie tallgrass, like a ghost or spirit passing over us. Something's wrong.

Anne and I look at each other, then look to the door, and we rise and rush to the hot tub. Ryan's face up in the water, jeans still on. He's passed out in the water. Anne covers her mouth. Then she melts, laughs.

"He went under, but floated to the top," she says.

"Hot tub miracle!" I say.

"Or dumb luck. The dope's still with us because he floats."

Hard to know what to do when your girl's in the bughouse. Don't imagine I can spring her out. But it's easy to know where to wait. I'm at 51st Street Coffee House. I sit at the bar and wait, hope none of Liz's beaus are here or will come in and say, "Hey, man, how's Little Red?" I sip chai and wait. August, and the summer's almost gone. I came looking for experience, and I've found plenty, Liz showing me through the city. I can make it to the mic and say something. I've kissed, I've loved. No sex yet, but maybe I don't need that. Touching may be enough. I wait an hour, and am about ready to scoot, when I see her. Liz comes in the front door carrying two overfull brown paper grocery bags full of clothes. She's disheveled, shaken. I jump up, go to her.

"Liz, honey."

"Oh Jamie. My parents put me in the bughouse. Fucks! Now I'm out."

"So good to see you."

"You, too, hon."

"What now?" I say.

"Can you get me a smoke?" she says.

"Sure. After that?"

"Can't go back to my parents. Those turncoats!"

"Where will you go?"

"Thought I'd stay at Suicide Hill."

"At night?"

"I'm a big girl."

"Come with me."

"What about that smoke?" she says.

I turn to the barista, say, "A pack of American Spirit."

Liz lugs her two brown bags, her shoulders slouching, sloping. She's tired, worn. Her head droops, her mane like a fallen autumn mum.

"Here, let me take those for you," I say.

"Thanks, sweets. Let's get a drink," she says, and into Gomer's Liquor we go. Moments later, and she has a six pack of Boone's in hand, pink drink, swinging, and I'm back on the bags, toting her stuff across the city, not knowing where we're going, but knowing we're going together somewhere.

"Where will you go? Archie's?" I say.

"No."

"Wanna stay with me?" I say.

"Your parents hate me."

"No they don't."

"No lies," she says.

"How about I get us a hotel for the night?"

"Like prom?" she says. "You go to prom?"

"Yes."

"How many times?"

"Twice."

"You big stud, you."

"Come with me," I say.

At the front desk, I'm filling in the names, filling in the papers. I start to write my parents' address in the "residence" section, but stop and scribble, "x" that out, and put my Twin Oaks address, less than a block from 51st Street Coffee, and Liz is squirming like she needs to piss or take a walk around the hotel, circle the building. I check my wallet for cash and have just enough. A credit card slip from here would raise a flag that my mother would see and question. When I turn to check Liz's expression, she's gone. I look. I look again.

The guy behind the counter, who's picking at his zits, pale with stop-light fire dots along his chins and cheeks, scratches his sandy colored soul patch goatee, like a wizened guru, says, "Your girl."

And "shit" is all I can say.

I turn and look around, search every room corner with my eyes, then notice the glass doors to outside are still shifting a little in the wind, as if someone has just gone out. Liz.

"Hold my room," I say, and I go quickly out into the night. I look left. I look right, and there's Liz marching the sidewalk in her bare feet, slapping concrete, one hand in her hair, tidying red locks in the wind. I catch up to her and take her lightly by the wrist, as a dancer might.

"Hey!" she says.

"Hey. Please. Come on."

"Oh, you big stud, you," she says.

"Really. Come on."

"You want me?"

"Always," I say.

"You love me?"

"Every day."

"Every night," she says. "Every night."

Liz and I shamble into the hotel room, and Liz dumps her brown grocery bags onto the bed, and we clank the Boon's bottles onto a table top, the bottles sweating. Liz says, "They labeled me hysterical," points to the pink carbon paper sheet, which I read, the check boxes: "mania," "hysteria," "paranoia," category any aware citizen, artist, grapples with. She wants to kiss, and we do, her lips hot on mine, her clothes also strewn about the bed in pinks and tans and greens, and when her hand goes to my belt I don't stop her. She has a few more words about her white-wall stay, says, "They even took away my light bulbs at night. Said I might cut myself. Cut myself? Fuck, I want to live!" saying that like a mantra. "Take me," she says. And I say, "One sec," and I fumble about my pants for the film canister. Loaded within was that condom I picked up in Fayetteville, Arkansas, that semester I lived there, tried to be a writer, and returned to drums. Scattered about the condom were Ganga, hemp seeds, a do-it-yourself. The condom, folded in half, kept with me for a year, should still be good, I think, I hope. I pinch the condom tip, when I put the rubber on. "Like a pro," Liz says.

"So, how was it?" Liz says.

"Like being in space," I say.

"Space?"

"Like being in outer space, floating."

"First time?"

"Sure 'nuff."

"You're lying," she says. "This isn't your first time."

"Sure is."

Liz stands. She has a crooked grin, but muted. She gives me her hand, and, as if a supplicant entering a temple guided by a priestess, I follow. Her bare feet move over carpet as if in a procession. All I can do, or want to do, is follow. The shower water shoots on, hot, and she leads me in. She unwraps the small, hotel soap, yellow in her hands. The water washes around and sudses, and she draws circles on my chest. Water washes, then, she kisses me in the solar plexus, puts her hands to my cheeks and draws me in for a kiss.

"Now you," she says, and sudses her shoulders and the long thin bones that lead from her shoulder to her neck, collar bones, then to her breasts, rosy like blooms, her belly, and beyond. It is better than sex, like a love feast of flesh. Done, Liz touches a hand to my chest again, says, "A few hairs here."

"Only a few?" I say.

"Don't get cocky," she says.

And she kisses me there again, at my center, says, "With each kiss a new hair will grow. You'll need them all one day."

Drowsy, we lie in each other's arms, naked, in bed. With a slender finger, Liz draws circles on my chest, looks at me as when our love first bloomed, a sun-yellow dandelion in a city sidewalk crack.

"Liz?" I say.

"Yes?"

"I hate to, but I need to go."

"Go?"

"Go home. Check in with my parents."

Liz's hand shoots up. Her eyes cut this way and that, to my face, to the wall, to the floor, her face working. Her brow comes down, and a pinch forms at the top of her nose, an incensed crease. "Really!"

"Sorry. I do," I say. "I'll just go for a few hours. Play dead, play sleep. Then come right back."

"Really!"

"Please don't be sore."

"Sure I'll be here when you get back?" she says. She pushes off my covers.

At home with my folks, the dawn light comes in through the curtains in golden fingers, in sunflower-petal rays. I lie on top of the covers, my hands behind my head. What a man wonders about had happened, I had eaten from the tree of good and evil, I'd had sex. And with a young woman of experience. This had not been some tryst in a closet or in a parents' bedroom, a party waning below. This had been in a hotel downtown with a fiery city girl, one who'd helped me, and for a moment of flame I, too, had helped.

I wait until I heard the coffee maker stop, say hi to my mother and father, take a piece of peanut-buttered toast, and leave. I pat my car hood as I go. The dark blue Blazer hood is still warm, like a new egg.

When I get back to the hotel, my body, like the car, is full of warmth. I look forward to gathering Liz in my arms and kissing her and settling back into cool sheets, but when I pull in, I jerk the car to a stop. On the sidewalk, hand in hand, Liz skips with a young blonde man, his hair spiked up with mousse. He looks her age, and city slick. Hers is a full grin, a lucky-in-love grin. The dawn, like a marigold, is all hers.

I stop, roll down the window, and she approaches. She is still grinning, but now like a pool shark, like someone who cannot lose.

"Don't be sore, Jamie," she says. "We had time left on the room."

"Liz!"

"You know me," she says.

"Bye, Jamie. Bye."

And she walks to him, takes blonde-boy's hand, and in they go, through the glass doors and into the hotel.

I pull away, my hands tight on the wheel. When I get to the Westport flea market, I pull over. I wipe the tears from my eyes. I wait until I no longer shiver, then pull out into traffic.

Lean sits in his parents' dim basement, his hands on the video game controller, a half moon with buttons, his eyes on two screens. One screen casts a bright glow depicting a desert with little green tanks blasting puffs of smoke across, fire and puffs, and the other screen is darkness and white skin, sometimes a back or a nipple. Lean watches porn and games, when his parents are out.

"You score, dude?" Lean says.

"How'd you know?" I say.

"Look at your cheeks. You're a fuckin' tomato, dude. Either you just ran a marathon or you scored."

I look around the basement, at the bodies tumbling on the screen, sinking, pistoning, and then at the desert full of pixel fire, tanks burning.

"I'm losing interest in this," I say. I make to go.

"Too big for video games?" Lean says. "Go back to your girl."

"Our girl gone?" John says.

I am back at 51st Street Coffee, slumped at the counter, sipping a dark iced chai, my lips at the glass cup lip. John, in his white khakis and bowler shirt and spiffy brown leather shoes, looks like he is always on vacation, or ready to shark me at pool.

"Seems so," I say.

"You know," he says, "she's no one's girl."

"That I know."

"She was only mine a little while," he says. "You, too. You know how this goes. Or are you new?"

I gulp. I think.

"Yep, you're new." John slaps me on the shoulder.

I'm at the window of EE's dance, looking in, and I can see Liz's hand on the back of an old liver-spotted man, a palm at his shoulder and at his hip, her nails painted orange-pink. I want to call out to her as she dances boxes, waltzes with that old old man in his dusty-colored tan suit. His shoes have spats, black and cream. He turns and turns her, pulls his tongue back in his mouth. I can just see his pleasure, through tiny teeth. Was that what she was like for me, that sweet-sour taste? No, much more, much much more.

Liz pats the old man on the chest, a quick passing touch, and takes up with a spiffy-suited hustler in a purple sports coat, someone in his 30s, someone like John, but not quite. She must see me looking, but does not glance back, and so she dances boxes, dances boxes, while I turn and go.

Back in the neighborhood, I run a slow hand over the Suicide Hill slide, its metal cold with evening. Below, the lights of 51st Street Coffee glow yellow, a frame, a porthole. If I look close enough, squint, I can see my cherry-colored Gretch set, framed there in the window, the drums I lifeguarded a whole summer to get. I've got my stick bag on me, the strap slung over a shoulder, and, though I'd like to brush a bit on this slide or tap out a cymbal call, I don't. I just stand and watch the night grow darker, turn from purple to indigo. This will be my first gig at 51st Street without her.

Ryan's humming words to "Moanin" while he strums his big brown upright bass, his face almost to the wall, the room's so small, but his eyes are closed, and his stubble's thick, like he's turning into some Iron John rusty mountain man. (He drinking again?) And he calls out for me to solo, "Talk on, James," his eyes still clamped shut, and so I enter his space, shut my lids and sail. My hands know where the drums are. The door opens and closes, I hear it, people coming in. I play across the drums in wild runs, full of rolls and paradiddles, stick heights high, then low, like Tony Williams does so well, digging into all of the drums and letting the cymbals rest, and I hear a creaking, a rocking, and, when I look up, it's Liz, rocking in her chair to my beat, and I look long at her, play for her body, drummer and dancer, the way it's been through thousands of years, the rhythm to move the body of another. And we're together again, until the tune kicks, and I return to the melody. But she continues to bop along. Ryan looks up, notices. ("Got your girl back.")

When the song ends, Liz marches to me, stuffs a paper stub into my front pocket and blows me a quick kiss. She swishes into the night, her yellow summer dress like a stream beside the street, rippling. I want to go after her, but we have at least three more tunes to play before this set ends.

The stub says 561-5415. I head to the payphone, the set complete, our instruments cold in the corner. I've got about 10 or 15 minutes before Ryan wants me back. I've got three quarters, and I send one coin into the slot.

"Hello, sweets," says Liz.

"How'd you know it was me?" I say.

"Who else knows my number?"

"Maybe half a dozen guys," I say.

"Don't be mean, Jamie. It doesn't suit you."

"Why'd you give me your number?"

"I'm worried. About the bug."

"Bug?" I say.

"That green monkey shit."

"AIDS?" I say.

"That's the one."

"Fuck!" I say.

"Let's go get tested together tomorrow."

"Really?"

"Really, sweets," she says. "For me. For us."

The Community Health Center is housed in a sad, old, yellow-brick building. Soot from earlier decades stains its upper reaches, so a shade that used to mirror an autumn sun now looks more like mustard or white living room walls stained yellow-orange by cigarette smoke. Here, though, the smoke's now from exhaust, the line of cars steady. Only when the light turns do the lines of wheeled metal pause and wait, in queue, as another line pours forth, as when a faucet's turned to full, and the stream of water seems to have no beginning and no end, as if the water is rope or wire, one thing, not a collection of many droplets shoved and bunched together. Sometimes, the sidewalk also pours with people, as when the bus approaches the stop and some need to catch up.

Against the yellow brick, a jagged shadow falls, indigo shade from a church spire. Even here, something watches us, something from above, if even made of brick and rock. It disarms me, but also is a little peaceful, this shadow of God against the building where I'll go to learn if I've earned an early death through my carelessness. Liz, too. It's our afternoon.

Liz takes my hand. Her hand is cool and small and pale, ivory-like in the afternoon sun. She never seems to heat up. She's like a river stone, always cool from the water in the shadows and the shallows.

"Sweetie, time to go in," she says.

"You sure we need this?" I say.

"Sure, I'm sure. We need to know."

"Do I want to know?"

"We both need to know," she says.

Liz's hand in my hand, we sit side by side in the waiting room at the clinic in mustard-colored chairs, the clinic decorated in that same yellow-brown color of the '70s, with splashes of dull rust and cool sea foam blues. It's as if we've stepped through a door and into an earlier, freer era. But the feeling here is not one of freedom, but stasis; not bell bottoms trotting along in a campus lawn breeze, but instead the cool antiseptic stillness of a placid, ageless, hospital place, a place of strung-potted ficus with green earlike leaves, so uniform you can't tell whether they're plastic or real, the only touch of life in an airless room.

A nurse in cool blues, her blouse over-long, squeaks in on chalk-colored hospital shoes, each step a beep-beep, a warning, as when a delivery truck backs up.

"James Keller?" she says, clipboard in hand.

I stand.

"Please come with me," and she turns, and I follow.

Now I'm alone in a white room. I look at my watch. The clock hands tick slow, circles spreading like water ripples, but slower, uniform. There's nowhere to go but round, and in.

An older woman, her gray hair streaked with white wisps, enters and puts a hand on my wrist.

"Any trouble with blood?" she says, flexing and snapping a blond strap, like a long, unlooped rubber band.

"No," I say. "None, so far."

"Good."

She cinches the band 'round my arm, pokes me with a metal spike connected to a short see-through tube. Blood runs the tube, filling from clear to burgundy-red. I look away, my forehead going cool. I stare at the wall, at a velum-colored diploma, "Dr. Richard Fitts, MD." The letters blur, "Dr. Richar—"

When I wake, I'm on a table, blank paper under my body. I see spots, like sun flares in photography shots. I see a face, the nurse's visage, her hair like angel tufts.

"Thought you had no trouble with blood."

"Sorry. Never before."

"There's always a first," she says.

"Guess so. Did you get enough blood?"

"We got plenty."

A round doctor in his 40s, with a calm energy and hair that recedes like a monk's, enters at a tight clip. He fingers his stethoscope loop, as if adjusting a tie.

"Sight of blood did a number on you, did it, young Mr. Keller?"

"Sure did," I say, a hand going to my tingling forehead.

The nurse leaves.

The doctor scratches his head.

"I'm here to give you advice and tips, information that can help save your life. HIV test?"

"Yes."

"How many sexual partners?"

"One," I swiftly say.

"How many times did you have sexual intercourse?"

"Just once."

"Use a condom?"

"Yes."

"Did it break?"

"No."

"Positive?"

"Yes. Positive."

"The test what brings you here?"

"We want to be sure."

"Only one way to know. The test. You seem like a responsible young man."

"Thanks."

The doctor opens his white lab coat and pulls three colorful pamphlets out. They're about STDs.

"Read these all the way through. And come back for your test results in ten days. And be safe. And, of course, everything here is confidential."

"Thanks, Doc. I appreciate it."

"Stay safe. And don't push your luck."

I return to the waiting room, my gait slow, head down. I work to look up.

Liz says, "We need to go wash this hospital off. Know where there's a lake or pond, some water?"

"I know a place," I say.

My hand is hot on the Blazer steering wheel, but I welcome the warmth, something to break me out of the hospital cold. Liz puts her hand on my thigh, squeezes, then takes her hand away.

"What do you think will happen to us?" I say.

"We'll live."

"I mean about the test," I say.

"We'll live. You worried?" She pushes her face forward and closes her eyes in the sun, basking. The freckles on her cheeks seem brighter in the light, honey-colored, rust-colored.

"More than ever."

She kisses me on the cheek, quick, and laughs.

"So is everything back like before?" I say.

"Never is."

"Why?"

"We've eaten from the fruit, sweetie," she says. "It never can be."

I drive back into Johnson County, past the developments where every house matches, mirrors the others, boxes with triangles on top painted some color between middle grey and sky blue. The lawns are shorn short and green and perfect as golf courses. There are swing sets and shiny bicycles and tricycles plopped in the lawn, and polished, waxed cars wait in the driveways, but no one ever seems to be outside.

Closer to Shawnee Mission Park, men in spandex hunch over their handlebars, foreheads into the wind, their street bike wheels spinning like pinwheels, their feet pumping at a measured pace. They're in no hurry, and up the hills they go. There are people here, women with kids in strollers. Older kids pull at strings that stretch into the sky, red kites swifting in the breeze. A black man holds a silver box in both hands, waves an antenna, and a little yellow plane veers and loops through the air.

I get us to the lot by the water's edge, the pavement grayed, the white parking lines almost indistinguishable from the lot. Right when I push the stick to park, Liz hops out without me. I look, then reach over and roll her window up, my hand making quick circles until the window synchs.

"Hey!" I call, but she seems to know where she's going. The car shut and locked, I follow. Down the thin dirt trail I go. When I get to the water's lip, Liz has already pulled off and hung her strawberry-colored dress on a low branch. She's in the water up to her knees, her pale skin like a cave fish's in the bright light.

"Wait up," I say. "What about fish hooks? Glass?"

"I walk the city sidewalks. This is nothing," she says.

Off goes her bra, which she flips to the water's edge, the shallows. The red of the bra looks out of place in the dark water.

"People fish here," I say.

"And I swim here."

Liz lifts one leg, then the other, in the water, a kind of ballet-like dance, removing her panties. They go, pink, next to the bra at the water's edge. I swiftly remove my shoes, my chinos, and step in. I scoop up her things and place them in the grass at the water's edge. Hers is an abandon I do not know.

"This isn't exactly how we do it in suburbia."

"How's that?" she says.

I look at her quick, absorbing the image. Venus-like, cherub-like, she stands in the water, now to her waist. She puts her hands up to the sun. She pushes forward in the water, the waves sloshing at her chest.

"We keep on our clothes. We swimsuit it."

In my tighty-whiteys, I take off my shirt, toss it to the grass.

"Not me. I'm all water," she says. "All in."

I step out to my waist, and she stands, flashing me.

"Miss me?" she says.

"Always."

She kisses me on the chest. Draws a circle with a fingertip around the kiss.

"You know this can't last," she says.

"Why not?"

She kisses me on the mouth, stops. "This is just a breakup kiss."

"A coda?" I say.

"That something they tack on at the end?

"Something like that. Why can't we come back together?"

"Jamie, you've seen too much."

She raises her hands, spins in the water. I want to watch her, like this, for hours.

On the patchwork blanket my grandmother pieced together, Liz and I sit. We talk about cameras, and she says she wants one, and I tell her she can borrow one of mine, and she says she wants her own camera, only hers, then she'll begin to shoot. I have two camera hand-me-downs, and, though I use them, I could part with one, for her.

"Got any more film?" Liz says.

"Sure. Oh, you mean—"

"Yes?" she says.

"Condoms."

"Exactemente!"

"I love you," I say, "but—"

"But what?"

"But, you know, where we just were. The risk."

"Live or don't live," she says, rising, pulling her dress up to her ankles to leave.

"But I want to *continue* to live. A long time."

"Then that's your slow death," she says.

"But—"

"No buts. Take me home."

"You mean, take you to Archie's?"

"You know what I mean."

Liz has her head, her red hair, in the wind, her passenger window all of the way down. She lets the car's wind pull one hand into sine waves, like surfers do, arm in the air. She doesn't look at me, seems to have forgotten.

"Liz, I'd really like to see you," I say.

She glances, then she's back into the rushing air, into the clouds.

"Don't you see me now?" she says.

"I mean regularly. Be with you."

"Thought you didn't want to *be* with me."

"You know what I mean."

"And you know what I mean," she says. "Girl's gotta have it."

"But what about that place, the tests?"

"Child's play."

"Then why did we go?"

"We're not kids anymore, Jamie. We can play, but we're not kids."

We're almost to Archie's, when Liz says, "Actually, Jamie, just leave me here."

I stop by the sidewalk. "Where?"

"The coffee shop," she says, pointing up the block. She leans in, before pulling out of the car, says, "One last kiss," and lays her wet lips on my cheek and holds.

"Now you're on your own," she says. "Good luck."

"I'll miss you," I say.

"You miss me already."

She turns and walks a block to the spot where we met. Going, it's as if I've never known her, as if a stranger walks ahead, just another city-goer, an attractive and magical woman with whom I might never exchange a word, a shadow, a stick figure, a silhouette receding into the glare and bright red and yellow spots of summer sun.

"Miss me?" Lean says.

"You know it, brother," I say.

"Your girl?" Lean tips his shades, looks with his eyes beyond the black plastic and false glass.

"Gone, gone, gone."

I thread a worm onto a hook. A little red string of blood streams from the hook tip, a small droplet.

"Man, you know I can't stand this," Lean says.

"This?"

"Any of this," Lean says. "Hooks, dirt, worms."

Lean pats his hands together, as if rubbing off dirt.

"Why?"

"Man, cold plastic's where it's at," Lean says. "A keyboard. A screen. No guts, no dirt."

I look at our red, rusty Folger's can of worms, its clear plastic lid in the grass, a tip of a worm auguring into the dark brown dirt, almost

Folger's rich and deep and dark. I'm glad I didn't bring a jar of chicken livers. For Lean, that would be just too much.

"But this is it," I say. "This is life, the earth." I touch the grass, run a hand along the face of the earth, dirt.

"To you."

"To humans," I say. "For centuries. Hundreds, thousands of years."

"We outgrew all that," Lean says.

"Outgrew? What's so good about cold plastic."

"It never argues, never talks back. Unlike my parents," says Lean.

"But what about love, passion?"

"My parents only argue, squabble, fight. I want none of it."

"But what about girls?" I say.

"I chat with plenty of girls online."

"But green text on a black background. Is it enough?"

"Enough for me," says Lean. "I've got magazines and videos for the rest."

I cast my line. The bobber hits the water's surface, sinks, and tops, wobbling, a white and red buoy or beacon. If I look closely, I can also see the line, a series of strung loops along the water's dark skin, invisible to fish, we think.

"Cast," I say. "Cast out your line and fish."

"You mean for girls? Look at you. Miserable."

"Just loved and lost."

"She might come back," Lean says.

"Don't think so."

"There'll be other girls. Live girls."

"Maybe," I say, "and they'll be better than pin-up pages and video girls. Your porn girls."

"Don't knock what you don't know."

Lean hands me his fishing pole.

"Here," he says. "You fish."

I air my dull aluminum tackle box in the sun, when I return home. I have my bare feet up in the orange sunset glow, leaning back in a deck chair. My father and I built this deck when I was 12. He hauled the redwood boards home in his blue pick-up truck, and we stole some of the stones for the wall beneath from the big housing projects down the block, when they were done setting and fitting stones. They would've just buried that rock.

My father opens the deck door and stomps in from the kitchen, his boots big and thick, a patina of gray concrete dust on their brown tops. He's in a button-up, Wrangler style sleeveless shirt, with the opal-like buttons. His arms are a deep tan, red and brown, and he's hairy, like a man that's meant to live outdoors, weather wind and rain.

"Son, we should go fishing."

"I just went fishing with Lean," I say.

"As father and son."

"I'd like that," I say.

"When?"

"I don't know. Kind of busy." I try to be easy with him.

"Too busy for your old man? Soul searching?"

"You could call it that."

"Soul searching takes time," he says. "Almost as much as getting over a girl."

"It does. How about we fish next Friday?"

"How 'bout tonight? Come with me."

"Aw, Dad."

"Ok. Next time. But come with me."

Father leads me down the steps to the end of the garden hose, nestled in a loose coiled circle at the side of the house. He points to the end of the hose.

"Let me show you something," he says.

"Sure."

"See this rubber?"

He pulls the rubber ring from out of the hose lip tip. It's a red-pink ring about the size and shape of a quarter, but only the coin's outer rim, mostly hole.

"That's the thing," he says. "Always have one on. You missing one, it leaks."

"Ok."

"Always make sure this here rubber's on, so it don't leak, cause problems. Got it?"

He replaces the rubber ring.

"Sure, Dad."

"You got me? Keep that rubber on. Prevent problems."

I sip an iced chai at 51ˢᵗ Street Coffee, my back to the door, trying to forget Liz. Or am I trying to remember? In the corner by the window, I first saw her. I played with more fire that night, behind the drums. I was playing for her. I can almost smell her, her rosewater scent.

I feel a small hand on my shoulder.

"Hi-ya, trigger," Liz says.

"Liz!"

"Miss me?"

"Always."

"We've got work to do," she says.

"Work?"

"Clean-up work. Come with me."

I follow her out onto the sidewalk. Her feet are pink and cream in the sun. She never tans. Shoeless, she skips. She takes my hand, skips again. She's graceful, dancing. It's as if she is a girl, effortless, light.

"Remember how?" she says.

"Don't know."

"Try. Remember. You can do it."

I pick up one foot, then the next. I shuffle forward. A few tries, and my body remembers, the feet and legs doing their thing, clumsily. We skip a few paces, kids, lovers.

"Good enough," she says, and swings our clasped fist as we move.

An old, but mint-condition black Lincoln pulls up, its engine rumbling, souped up. The pitch black tinted window slides down. A young black hood with silver teeth and silver shades heckles.

"Yeah, Dorothy," he says. "Get it. Skip that yellow brick road."

Liz turns and laughs, flips her wrist, a wave.

He pulls away, his tail pipe like a smoking cigar. She's made his day.

The yellow brick of the Community Health Center seems sick, pale, diseased. Liz and I go in and come out. They hand us each a slip of paper, have us sign a clipboard sheet.

Out in the sun, I breathe easy. I let the sun warm my forehead. I let my belly go in and out, take full breaths.

"What'd you get?" I say.

"You first," she says.

"Please."

"You," she says.

"Negative," I say. "That's good, isn't it?"

"Means you don't have it," she says.

"You?"

"Nevermind," she says. "Bye."

She skips, her feet and body light.

I chase after her, but she boards a bus, mounts the stairs quick, two at a time. She's just in time, and the bus pulls out, turns into traffic. There's no catching her.

Lean's car is parked in his parents' driveway with all of the doors and trunk open, a gray Camry. Thin copper wires run from inside to outside of the car. Metal tools litter the driveway: a wrench, pliers, a socket set. A big black wooden box with speakers sits beside the car, upended. It's a homemade car stereo "boom-boom" booster system.

"Can you hold that wire for me?" Lean says.

"This one?"

"Yes. The one right beside you."

"How long?"

"Just until I get this subwoofer back to you. Don't pull."

"Got it. What are you doing, turning your car into a big boom box?"

"You could call it that."

"Like to get a rise out of cops?" I say. "Impress high school girls?"

"Yeah. All that. And more."

Lean lugs the big black, spray-painted box back to me, takes the wire from my hand, and places the box into the trunk, all wired up.

"Nice box," I say.

"Made it myself."

Done, Lean goes to the driver's seat and turns the ignition key halfway, turning on the stereo. The stereo roars to life. We go to the trunk, where the stereo speakers pound and pump music, the round, puddle-like speakers rippling with sound, playing something loud and active and vanilla, something I don't know. Is it Rush, Pantera, Dream Theater?

"They move," I say.

"When they work, they do," he says.

I put a finger to my ears.

"Kind of loud."

"What?" Lean says.

"Kind of loud."

"What was that?"

Lean puts a hand on my shoulder, grins.

"Just joshin' ya."

Lean turns down the stereo.

I touch the knob of Lean's car's stick shift. It's a golf ball. Written on the ball, it says "Ultra 7."

"Nice shifter," I say.

"Put that on myself. You should see Monica and me shift it. She pulls the knob, and I do the feet. All at once. Perfectly. In synch."

"Couples shift."

"Call it what you want," he says.

"You that into golf?"

"Am now. I caddie at Elysian Fields."

"Really? Big place."

"Big pay."

"How much?"

"Thirty bucks for 9 holes. Plus, cash for stray balls. Three dollars a piece for Ultras."

"How many do you find?"

"Ten to fifteen a round. Sometimes more. Enough golf, James. What about your girl?

"Gone, gone."

"You take that test?" Lean says.

"Yeah."

"You ok?"

"I'm negative," I say.

"Don't got it? Good. Fuck, you lucked out."

"Guess so."

"She get it?"

"Don't know."

"Really?"

"No. I think she got it. I think—"

"Lucky's what you are, bro."

"Lucky. With a condom," I say.

"Only way to go."

"But what about her?" I say.

"Fuck her."

"You know, you can be a real ass, Lean."

Lean cranks the stereo.

"So. Hop in."

About a week later, Lean has me dressed in a white knit polo-type shirt, with the thick ridged collar, and khaki shorts. We hop out of Lean's car, careful not to bump doors with the new red Porsche beside us in the lot. Elysian Fields is one of KC's finest golf courses and sparkles with a veneer of riches. White fences border immaculate greens. Sprinklers tap-tap-tap water in the distance, the sprinkler heads small and hidden, only the tufts of white water can be seen. Men in golf-wear trot about, the plaid patterns harkening back to Scotland, land of golf. The men carry red golf bags full of shiny clubs. Thin, prim, straight-backed waitresses deliver white plates of fine food at the club house. I think I can smell the steak with its pink center. Men check expensive silver wristwatches, the clock faces flashing in the sun. The men lean back, spotless, and soak up time.

"Straighten that collar out, bro," Lean says.

I adjust my collar, pull the ridge down, keeping the collar from popping.

"You want to look good, put together," he says. "You'll get better tips."

"You sure I can do this? What do I know about golf?"

"Watch and learn."

There are ten of us caddies, all in our late teens and early twenties, sitting cross legged on a spot of green that fringes the club house. The lead caddie, Rich, is in his early 30s it seems, and he sports a Kennedy pompadour hairdo. He's dressed like us, but in red, and his threads a littler richer, to go with this name, and instead of shorts he wears long white pants, the type you see pros wear sometime on the green.

"Remember," says Rich, "always stand parallel to your golfer, eye to eye, opposite the ball."

He's got a ball on the grass, a club hung along his shoulder, a putter, but a good one, with the thick, tailored head.

"What about behind him, out of the way?" someone from the circle says.

"You get a bad golfer," says Rich, "he might lose his club, and then you might get it in the noggin. Stand like this," says Rich. "Here, you help me demonstrate."

The young caddie stands right across from Rich, while Rich practice swings his club. The two are eye to eye, but about 12 feet apart, like two telephone poles, upright and separate, parallel. Then Rich points his club in angles, tries to get at the young caddie.

"See how I can't hit him, whatever I do? Be like him."

About half an hour passes like this. We learn and re-learn the ropes.

Rich says, "Let's review. Birdie?"

"One under par," someone says.

"Bogey?"

"One over par."

"Eagle?"

"Two under par."

"Double bogey?"

"Two over par."

"Double eagle?"

"Three under par."

"Another name for double eagle?"

"Albatross."

"Very good," Rich says.

I shake my head. I can't remember any of this.

So, I'm at the tee with Alan Rose, a hard-nosed guy in his mid-60s, a retired banker, they say. I stand opposite him, carrying his bag. Only old guys use caddies, old guys and guys with too much money. The rest take carts, drive their bags from hole to hole. Alan has a friend with him, a fat man who chomps sunflower seeds at the edge of the tee box. Both wear spiffy, absurd, plaid golf uniforms, in reds and greens and yellows, like clowns from a Brooks Brothers circus.

"Keep your eye on that ball, boy," Alan says. "Watch it go."

"Yes, sir," I say.

Alan tops the ball, which torpedoes along the top of the grass and travels only about 50 yards out.

"Shizer," he says. He tees up another ball, quick, says, "Let's say that didn't happen."

The fat friend holds out his hand, and Alan hands him a hundred dollar bill. He's lost his first bet of the day. The head caddie told us, "No betting," but warned us to look away, when someone does.

At the fifth hole, Alan sets a nickle near the pin, the flag waving in the wind, and waits for his friend to catch up. His friend is caught in the trees, but he's almost out. Only one tree blocks his shot. He squares up. He pulls back his club, but then he slips in the foliage, almost falling. He catches himself, like a circus bear acrobat, but the club smacks into the tree trunk, low, by the base. He holds up the club, which is bent like a V.

"Sorry. Shit, Alan," he says.

"That's a Callaway club," says Alan.

"Sorry."

"You don't know what you're doing, do you?" Alan says.

"It's been a while," he says. "Some rust."

"You're the frickin' Tin Man in rain. You're all rust. That was a thousand-dollar club."

"Sorry," he says. "I'll get you back."

"You bet you will."

Alan picks up his nickel, placing his ball where the coin was. He misses an easy putt, rimming the hole. The ball rolls, stops. He misses again. Again, the ball turning from the hole's lip, as if magnetic, as if repelled. Six putts later, Alan sinks it.

"Fuck!"

I trot over to wash Alan's ball, my white towel in hand. I'm about three yards from Alan, when he fast-pitches the ball at me, hard. I flinch, but catch the ball.

"There you are, boy," Alan says. "Now make it clean."

I rub at the ball, scrub the green, the tan, the dirt; dejected.

Back at the caddie clubhouse, Lean washes a handful of golf balls by hand, white-toweling them. I watch, slumped.

"I don't think this is for me," I say.

"What happened?" Lean says.

"Alan Rose threw his ball at me. Hard."

"That guy's a jerk."

"You're tellin' me. He always like that?"

"Pretty much."

"Riches!" I say.

"Riches will do that for you."

"I'm out," I say.

Rich strolls up to us. Lean hands Rich a handful of golf balls, and the lead caddie pulls a wad of money-clipped bills from his pocket and hands Lean a sheaf of ones.

I get up and walk to the car, marching hard. Lean follows.

"Come on, man," Lean says. "Give it another shot. Think of all of that green, the crisp dollars in your wallet."

"Thanks for the shot," I say, "but I'm no rich man's *boy*. I'm out. You can keep your bourgeois."

"Boosh-wah-whatever. Big word."

"Rich fucks."

"Call 'em what you want," Lean says. "I'll take their dough. Spends the same."

"You go ahead. I'm out."

"Suit yourself," Lean says.

I knock on Liz's door. Her mother answers, her arms crossed, her expression tired. She shakes her head. No Liz.

I ring Archie's doorbell. He answers, opens the door.

"She's gone, trigger," he says. "Tough luck."

"Where?"

"Gone, gone, gone. Maybe Missou. She has old friends there. In school."

"Why'd she go?"

"When she wants, she leaves."

"She coming back?" I say.

"Don't think so. She packed her things, left her room."

"She say anything?"

"Only this," says Archie. "She said, 'Tell Jamie I'm positive.' Positive of what?"

"I miss her."

"Get used to it."

At Grinder's, the slam emcee gestures to me: *Come on stage*. A cone of white light waits, a microphone, and a stand, silver in the light.

"Let's give a hand for young James Keller, second time out. A solo rider tonight." The emcee turns to me, whispers, "Kid, watch out for those first few curves."

I step up to the mic, ready to read and say, "If you see Liz O'Malley, tell her I miss her," knowing all I have left are words. Lots of words.

Words of Thanks

A big thanks to Jason Ryberg--poet, writer, editor, publisher, literary force. Thanks for publishing this book.

Thanks go to Linzi Garcia for curating this novella. Without your help, these words would not be here in print.

Thanks to Eric Sonnakolb for the great cover design work. Thanks to Dave Leiker for the photography work. You guys make things look great. (And sometimes you can judge a book by its cover.)

Thanks also to my parents, Joyce and Gary Rabas, for their enduring love and support. Thanks also to my mom for her copy editing help, although any lingering errors are mine. I unknowingly introduced them.

Thanks to Lisa and Eliot. Thanks to Alicia. Thanks to Dennis Etzel Jr, my poetic brother and constant friend and pen pal.

Thanks to Joe DeLuca. Thanks to Thomas Fox Averill and Dennis Etzel Jr. for the blurbs. Thanks to Adrienne K. Goss, a good friend and an early reader of this book. Thanks to Amy Sage Webb. Thanks to Max McCoy, who read this story in its screenplay version. Thanks to Mel Storm, Kevin Kienholz, Kat O'Meara, Rachel Spaulding, and the EMLJ crew of colleagues. Thanks to Steve Catt. Thanks to Bob Dean, friend and pen pal. Thanks to Jeanette Powers, Brandon Whitehead, Sharon Eiker, and Will Leathem. Thanks to Tyler Sheldon. Thanks to Richard Warner. Thanks for Val Bontrager and Laura Cossey. Thanks to Julie Mulvihill, Tracy Quillin, Murl Riedel, Valerie Mendoza, Leslie Daugharthy, Abigail Kaup, Leslie Von Holten, and the other good folks at Humanities Kansas. Thank you to Courtney Sleezer. Thanks to Mike Graves. Thanks to Curtis Becker and Kerry Moyer. Thanks to Mark Valentine. Thanks to Al Ortolani. Thanks to Larry and Linda McGurn.

Current Influences

MUSIC: Charlie "Bird" Parker (Live at Storyville and Jazz at Massey Hall), John Coltrane (Both Directions at Once: The Lost Album and Giant Steps), Keith Jarrett ("U Dance"), Madeleine Peyroux (Half the Perfect World), Miles Davis (Kind of Blue), Patty Griffin (Children Running Through), Chris Hazelton's Boogaloo 7 (The Basement Beat and Soul Jazz Fridays), and Lisa Moritz (Dream of Blue and Holding Time).

BOOKS ON TAPE: Laura Moriarty (The Chaperone), Bailey White (Quite a Year for Plums), and Michael Ondaatje (Anil's Ghost).

BOOKS: Tracy K. Smith (Wade in the Water), Mary Karr (Tropic of Squalor), Stephen Karam (The Humans), Kevin Young (Brown and Blue Laws), Aimee Nezhukumatathil (Oceanic), Traci Brimhall (Rookery), and Tasha Haas (Certain Dawn, Inevitable Dawn and The Garden of Earthly Delights).

Past Poet Laureate of Kansas (2017-2019) Kevin Rabas teaches at Emporia State University, where he leads the poetry and playwriting tracks and chairs the Department of English, Modern Languages, and Journalism. He has twelve books, including Lisa's Flying Electric Piano, a Kansas Notable Book and Nelson Poetry Book Award winner. He is the recipient of the Emporia State President's and Liberal Arts & Sciences Awards for Research and Creativity, and he is the winner of the Langston Hughes Award for Poetry.